BOOK ONE ☆ UNSINKABLE

TITANIC

BOOK ONE

UNSINKABLE

GORDON KORMAN

Scholastic Inc.

NEW YORK   TORONTO   LONDON   AUCKLAND

SYDNEY   MEXICO CITY   NEW DELHI   HONG KONG

FOR JAY

☆

ISBN 978-0-545-12331-0

12 11 10 9 8 7 6 5 4 3   11 12 13 14 15 16/0

Printed in the U.S.A.   40
First printing, May 2011

The text type was set in Sabon.
Book design by Tim Hall

PROLOGUE

RMS *CARPATHIA*
MONDAY, APRIL 15, 1912, 9:30 A.M.

They stood four deep on the afterdeck of the *Carpathia*, chilled to the bone, staring out at nothing.

Dark water, light swells — no evidence that barely seven hours before, the largest and most magnificent ship the world had ever seen had sailed here in all her glory. The truth was nearly impossible to believe: The RMS *Titanic* lay at the bottom of the sea, along with everyone who sailed in her, save the 706 souls rescued and now aboard the *Carpathia*.

"Look!"

The cry energized the exhausted throng. A flash of color among the endless waves. A survivor?

And then the swell turned over the item that stirred their frozen hearts with momentary hope. A deck chair. Nothing more.

How could this be? The *Titanic* was more than a steamship. She was a floating city, a sixth of a mile in length and 90 feet abeam, 66,000 tons gross displacement. Was this piece of flotsam all that was left? How could so much have become so little?

A uniformed steward — no more than seventeen years old — tried to take the arm of a lady who was shivering in the folds of a Cunard Line blanket.

"There's tea and soup below, ma'am," he said. "Please come out of this cold and wind."

She shook him off, mindless of his attempted kindness. "Go away. We have just seen our husbands drown."

The young seaman bit his tongue. She would probably take no comfort in knowing that, of the 1,517 passengers and crew lost in this tragedy, very few lives had been snuffed out by drowning. The sea that had swallowed their ship was 28 degrees Fahrenheit, well below the freezing point of freshwater. What the victims had suffered was unimaginable, as if their entire bodies had been suddenly packed in ice. Shock would have set in after barely sixty seconds. Next, unconsciousness, followed swiftly by death. No human could survive more than a few minutes in water that was as cold as the ice that had ripped open the belly of the great ship.

That ice was very much in evidence around the

Carpathia. The horizon was dotted with distant bergs and, to the north, pack ice.

Many ships had encountered ice on the North Atlantic crossing the previous night. All but one had survived. The greatest of them all.

The unsinkable *Titanic.*

CHAPTER ONE

BELFAST
Wednesday, March 27, 1912, 2:12 p.m.

The punch struck Paddy square in the jaw, rattling his teeth. It hurt more than he expected — more than it *needed* to hurt. He wasn't even acting when he staggered backward into the man in the houndstooth cloak.

A slim white hand slipped out of the boy's ragged sleeve and found its way into the cloak's patch pocket. It emerged a split second later, the small fingers deftly clutching a gold money clip fat with banknotes. That, too, disappeared, flicked under his threadbare jacket.

The man shoved him away, growling, "Keep your brawling from decent people, boy!"

Paddy suppressed a grin. He always enjoyed it when the mark helped out by sending him off with the stolen purse. By the time the rich fool realized he'd been robbed, Paddy would be far away, counting the windfall.

All that remained was to finish the street theater that had provided cover for the theft. He lunged at Daniel, burying his fist in his partner's stomach — revenge for that haymaker to the jaw.

"I'll do you for that!" Daniel wheezed.

Then, like so many times before, Paddy fled the scene, Daniel in hot pursuit, bellowing threats. The crowd parted to let them go, as if the passersby were their accomplices, and the horse-drawn buggies and electric trolleys had been placed there as obstacles to aid their escape.

The pair kept running, dashing down side streets and through the back lanes they knew so well. At last, they collapsed against each other, laughing and celebrating their success.

"Curse your evil heart, Daniel Sullivan!" Paddy cried. "Were you trying to break my jaw? I'll be black and blue for a week, thanks to you!"

"It can only make you handsomer," Daniel chortled, rubbing his stomach. "You talk like you didn't just knock the breath out of me. If I can't run away, who are you going to start your next dustup with? Yourself?"

"To listen to your whining," Paddy bantered, "you'd think I couldn't get along without you. With you clapped up in jail, this fat purse would be all mine."

He took out the money clip, and the two examined their prize.

Daniel's eyes bulged. "I didn't know the Prince of Wales was walking down Victoria Street!"

Paddy nodded. "This is a fortune!"

They fell silent, counting the haul over and over again. They were accustomed to worn purses containing a few meager coins. But the clip held twelve crisp banknotes worth one pound sterling each. This was enough money to replace their rags with warm clothing and proper shoes. It would keep their always-empty bellies full for a long time.

Paddy caught his breath first. "If I'd known about this, I'd have had his watch, too! And maybe the gold out of his teeth!"

At fifteen, Daniel was a year older than Paddy and considered himself more worldly. "We'll have no easy time spending these," he predicted. "When the likes of us hands over a brand-new banknote, there's not a shopkeeper in Belfast who won't know we stole it."

That wasn't what Paddy wanted to hear. "Are you saying we fell on a king's ransom, and it's worthless to us? Maybe you're afraid to spend it, but I'm not."

Daniel tried to be patient. "Think, Patrick. What kind of man likes his money in paper notes printed by a bank? Someone who's got so much of it he'd need a barrow just to carry the silver. When you spy your reflection in a window, do you see that person?"

Paddy was stubborn. "I'm going to be that person someday, so this will be good practice."

Daniel threw his hands up. "I'm just saying we should be careful. And if you had half the brains God gave geese, you'd know it."

They argued often, but never with lasting effect. Despite all their insults and bickering, Paddy Burns and Daniel Sullivan had been closer than brothers since the day they'd met. It was a bond forged by friendship, but also by something darker. Daniel was an orphan who had fled the life of a chimney sweep's climbing boy. Paddy had walked sixty-seven miles to Belfast after the last whiskey-driven beating he intended to endure from his stepfather. There was no question that each was all the other had in the world.

They stashed the money in their secret hiding place behind a loose brick in an ancient wall — "There are pickpockets and footpads out there," Paddy reminded his friend. "Look what happened to the gentleman who used to own all this lovely money."

Then they headed back toward the most crowded part of the city — Queens Island, home of Harland and Wolff, the largest shipyard in the world. It was a hub of activity, with more than fifteen thousand employees working shifts around the clock. All Belfast seemed to orbit this center. It was a pickpocket's dream.

The boys watched from across the road as a trolley let off dozens of passengers. Paddy's eyes settled on a short, squat man whose overcoat bulged where a purse might be carried.

Daniel read his friend's mind. "No, not him. Look how down-at-the-heel his boots are. He needs the money."

The two had an informal agreement never to make a victim of a poor man — even though they themselves were always much, much poorer. Their unfortunate situation forced them to live by their wits and steal to survive. But there was a line they would not cross, knowing that they weren't the only hungry youngsters in Belfast. Besides, there were plenty of peacocks, plump in the pocket, just waiting to be plucked.

And there's one right now, thought Paddy.

The gentleman stepping down from the hansom cab wasn't dressed so differently from the other men on the street — in a tweed coat, a suit, and a bowler hat. Yet every article seemed pressed and perfect, down to the elegant knot of his silk cravat. There was a quiet confidence to his bearing, a sureness to his step. And, Paddy guessed, a fullness to the purse concealed by his overcoat.

With an almost imperceptible signal to his friend, he fell in line behind the new mark, heading toward the shipyard gate.

"No!" rasped Daniel, rushing to keep pace. "Don't you know who that is?"

Paddy nodded vigorously. "A proper swell who can well afford to part with a few coins for our favorite charity."

"That's Mr. Thomas Andrews, the designer of the *Titanic*!"

Paddy was impressed. Even though the name Thomas Andrews meant nothing to him, a fellow would have to be deaf and blind not to know about the *Titanic*, the world's greatest ocean liner, under construction right here at Harland and Wolff. Those four towering smokestacks dominated the Belfast landscape. There was hardly a spot in the city where they couldn't be seen.

Paddy and Daniel had first met in the enormous crowd that had gathered to watch the launch from dry dock a year earlier. Paddy had been there to help himself to a purse or two. But as he watched the massive hull sliding down the ramp and into the Belfast Harbor, he'd forgotten the emptiness in his pockets and his stomach. It — *she* — Daniel constantly corrected him that ships were always *she* — was a dazzling sight.

The *Titanic* had only grown more magnificent as she lay in her slip to be fully outfitted. It was said that neither a millionaire's mansion nor a king's palace was more lavishly appointed than this mistress of the sea.

And, Paddy reminded himself, had it not been for the *Titanic*, he would not have tried to pick Daniel's pocket on that launch day. Then he would have been alone, or perhaps even dead. So he owed Mr. Thomas Andrews that much.

Just before the main gate, Andrews suddenly wheeled on them. "If you two young gentlemen have your eyes on my purse, you'd best know that I'll not part with it easily."

It was the first time that anyone had referred to Paddy Burns as a gentleman, and possibly the last time anyone ever would.

"Mr. Andrews, sir" — Daniel was nervously worshipful — "is it true that the fourth smokestack is a fake?"

The shipbuilder looked surprised, and then he smiled. "Does the heart of an engineer beat inside that thin chest? Wherever did you hear about that?"

Paddy spoke up. "Daniel reads, Mr. Andrews. He even taught me a little." Daniel's interest in books and newspapers had bewildered Paddy at first. Why risk arrest to steal something that couldn't put food in your belly? Now he saw that Daniel's passion for reading was a hunger just as urgent as an empty stomach. Paddy didn't understand it — not yet, anyway. But he knew it to be true.

"Impressive," Andrews approved. "Well, boys, the fourth smokestack is not connected to the boilers, but you could hardly call it a fake. It provides ventilation. And, of course, it is a recognizable feature of both the *Titanic* and her sister ship, the *Olympic*."

Daniel's thin, pale face was almost alight with interest. "And she's truly unsinkable?"

The shipbuilder chuckled. "Anything made of metal has the potential to sink. But see if you can understand this: *Titanic*'s hull is divided into sixteen compartments. At the touch of a single button on the bridge, the captain can close watertight doors, sealing those compartments from one another." He paused. "She can remain afloat with any four of those sixteen compartments flooded. It's safe to say that no one can envision an accident that would do more damage to her than that."

"I can!" Daniel exclaimed eagerly.

Andrews's eyes widened. "Do tell."

"Well, I — I don't know it right now, sir," Daniel stammered in embarrassment. "But if you'll give me a little time, I'm sure something will occur to me."

The shipbuilder seemed amused, but also intrigued. "It might at that," he agreed with a smile. "And if it does, I should be very interested to hear it."

"He can do it, too!" Paddy put in. "Daniel's really smart!"

Andrews's smile grew wider. "Then I shall direct my staff that if a Master Daniel and companion should come calling, they are to be brought to me at once."

The guard at the gate blocked the boys' way. "Be off, you two!" he shouted. "And stop bothering Mr. Andrews!"

The shipbuilder made a point of shaking both boys' grubby hands. "It's all right, Joseph," he said. "We were discussing business." He tipped his bowler hat to them. "Gentlemen. I trust we'll meet again." And he disappeared into the bustling yard.

Paddy and Daniel stood there long after he was gone, astonished that such a great man had treated two street lads with kindness and respect.

CHAPTER TWO

LONDON
FRIDAY, MARCH 29, 1912, 11:45 A.M.

Piccadilly Circus was always one of the busiest areas of London. But today, busy was an inadequate description. Hundreds of horse-drawn carriages and automobiles powered by gasoline, steam, and electric motors were locked at a standstill in the roundabout. Klaxons honked, bells rang, and angry drivers and coachmen bellowed their frustrations at top volume. The traffic extended up the five main streets that fed the circle, especially choking crowded Regent Street. The cacophony of protest grew louder and louder. No one was going anywhere.

The cause of this huge disruption to London life was perched on the pedestal of the statue of Eros at the center of the roundabout. Mrs. Amelia Bronson of Boston, Massachusetts, the famous American suffragist, was holding a rally in the place where she knew it would draw the most attention. Her strident voice, directed by a large cone megaphone, rose above the general din.

"*Votes for women!*" she thundered, provoking a chant from the mass of female humanity, resplendent in the colors of their movement: purple, white, and green.

"*Votes for women!*" they shouted back, making the air ring with their demand.

"Move out of the road, you shameless baggage!" bellowed a lorry driver.

Other cries echoed his sentiments, their words not so polite. London saw its share of political activism for a wide variety of causes, but not from women, who were expected to be obedient and demure. The "suffragettes" were considered unfeminine, rebellious, and even immoral. The crowd was growing ugly.

Fourteen-year-old Sophie Bronson reached up and tugged at the hem of her mother's dress. "Mother —" she said in a low voice. And was ignored. "Mother —" A little louder.

"Not now, Sophie. Things are escalating."

"I know they are," her daughter replied. "This isn't like Boston or Hartford or Providence. You can feel the rage in the air!"

"That rage is the tool men use to cling to an out-moded system where half the population is kept as second-class citizens!"

"Mother, you know as well as I do that most of *this* rage is from people who only wish to get on their way past Piccadilly Circus."

Sharp whistle blasts bit into the chill air.

"Here come the police!" Sophie exclaimed. "You're going to be arrested again!"

"I'm counting on it." Amelia Bronson beamed. "I didn't journey all the way to England to be ignored by the papers!"

Sophie groaned. "Then everything they say about you will be true. You really *are* a radical foreign agitator."

"I am what I need to be for the good of our move-ment" was Amelia's stalwart reply.

The bobbies came upon the throng — dozens of them, arresting the women en masse, shouting and shoving them roughly.

Amelia Bronson jumped down from the pedestal, held her arms out in front of her, and declared, "Go ahead, clap me in irons! Show the world and your own wives and your own mothers how you hate women!"

"Got nothing against women, mum," said one

constable in a strained voice. "It's American trouble-makers what gives me a problem."

He made to shackle her wrists, and a large English-woman ripped off his helmet by the chinstrap and began beating him with it. The constable wheeled on her and brought his truncheon down on the top of her head.

Sophie had resolved to stay out of the fray. Back at home in Boston, her father had assigned her such duties as keeping her mother out of prison and bailing her out of jail. But when Sophie saw the blood running down the face of the suffragist who had tried to defend Amelia Bronson, a red haze descended over her vision. She attacked the constable, leaping onto his back and wrapping her arms around his head. Her arrest followed hard upon.

Later, in the horse-drawn paddy wagon, Sophie was forced to endure the further humiliation of criticism from her mother as the prisoners all sat chained together by the ankles.

"Sophie, I'm very disappointed in you. You know better than this."

Sophie stared at her mother. "You were arrested, too!"

"That was necessary for us to get the publicity we require for our movement," Amelia Bronson lectured.

"It was a calculated decision made long before that policeman arrived on the scene. What you did was dangerous and unnecessary. It added nothing to the cause. And it will be very difficult for you to post my bond when you, too, are in a cell."

Sophie shut her eyes and held her tongue. To the rhythm of the hoofbeats on the cobblestones, she counted the days until April 10, when she would finally get her mother out of England. She could never have imagined how difficult it would be to keep Amelia Bronson free of trouble without Father on hand. The only thing that kept her going was the anticipation of the exciting trip home. In less than two weeks, they would be sailing on the newest, largest, and most spectacular ship in the world, the RMS *Titanic*.

CHAPTER THREE

SOUTHAMPTON
Sunday, March 31, 1912, 9:40 a.m.

Posters of the *Titanic* adorned all four walls in the offices of the White Star Line — every conceivable image, from photographs of the shipbuilding process, through artists' renditions of glorious ballrooms and dining saloons, to advertisements boasting of the luxury brand of soap used in the first-class water closets.

With the maiden voyage a scant ten days away, the place hummed with activity. People thronged the third-class ticket desk in search of last-minute passage, and the chatter of different languages filled the air as foreigners struggled to make themselves understood.

At the opposite end of the building, White Star officials were hiring hordes of waiters, stewards, maids, and laundry and kitchen workers. The *Titanic* offered features that had never been dreamed of on other ships. Employees were required to perform dozens of onboard functions, like trainers for the gymnasium and attendants for the swimming pool and Turkish bath. When the great ship set sail on April 10, she would carry nearly nine hundred crew members, most of whom would have nothing to do with the nautical operation of a ship.

One visitor, though, had business completely unrelated to the pride of the White Star Line. He was the youngest person in the office, thin and round-shouldered, practically swimming in a worn overcoat with patched elbows and frayed cuffs.

Fifteen-year-old Alfie Huggins stood at the paymaster's wicket with his certificate of birth unfolded on the counter.

"According to company records," said the clerk, looking down at him through thick glasses perched on the end of his nose, "your father's pay goes to" — he squinted at the ledger in front of him — "Sarah Huggins."

"That's my ma," Alfie explained, pointing out the name on the certificate.

"Well, just send her around and she can sign for the money."

Alfie's face fell. "I can't."

"Why not? Is she ill?"

"She's gone."

"Gone? You mean dead?"

"Gone. And she's not coming back."

It was a tough thing to admit. Who knew why his mother had married his father in the first place? John Huggins was a stoker for the White Star Line. His wife was dreamy and silly and romantic, and her husband was away at sea all the time, leaving her with a young son to raise.

"And what's your name again?" the clerk prompted.

"Alfie — Alphonse." He indicated the paper once again. Ma was exactly the kind of person to name her only child after the hero in one of the French penny novels she loved so well.

And where is she now? he wondered wistfully. Try as he might, he could not bring himself to stay mad at her for deserting him. For some reason, he pictured her crossing the continent on an exotic and glamorous train. The truth was probably more like a milliner's shop in London, trimming hats with artificial flowers and braid. Whatever it was, he hoped she was happy.

The clerk's voice interrupted his reverie. "I'm sorry, lad. Your name isn't anywhere on these instructions. I can't pay you."

Alfie swallowed hard. "But how am I to feed myself, sir? I have no money at all."

The clerk was sympathetic but firm. "It says here that your pa is signed on to the *Titanic*. Several of the *Olympic*'s engine crew are laying over in Belfast until the new ship is ready to sail. He should be here on Wednesday."

Three days! Alfie's heart soared. Of course, he would be proper hungry by then. But at least Da was coming home.

Still, if he was now part of the *Titanic*'s crew, he'd be gone again — Alfie checked one of the posters — on April 10.

And this time I'll be alone like a dog in the street.

His eyes fell on the line of hopefuls waiting to be interviewed for the *Titanic* jobs.

When the solution came to him, it seemed so obvious it was a wonder he hadn't thought of it sooner.

How do you stay with a seafaring father?

By sailing the same seas on the same vessel.

He folded up his certificate and stuffed it far into his pocket. Now all he had to do was lie a little about his age. . . .

CHAPTER FOUR

BELFAST
TUESDAY, APRIL 2, 1912, 3:30 P.M.

It had once been a printer's shop — the ink-stained tables, metal rollers, and loose type attested to that. But to Paddy and Daniel, it was home.

This was not due to the comforts — there were none. It was because the missing bricks in the wall outside provided the footholds to climb to the fire stairs, which rendered convenient access to the loose board covering what had once been a window. The Palace Gate, they called it. The shop was no palace, but it was shelter from cold and damp weather. And it was a place of their own, which was more than two destitute street youths had any right to expect.

One feature of the print shop was a large stack of paper, very dusty, but only slightly yellowed. Daniel was always sketching. In a different world, Paddy was certain, his friend would have become a famous inventor or designer.

Right now, Daniel was completely focused on his promise to Thomas Andrews. He was going to dream up a way for the unsinkable *Titanic* to sink — or he was going to die trying. For the past five days, he had thought of little else. At eight o'clock tonight, the great ship was scheduled to leave Belfast for Southampton, England, the starting point of her much-anticipated maiden voyage. Mr. Andrews would be sailing with her. In all likelihood, if Daniel could not come up with something before then, he would never see the man again.

Paddy could not quite grasp what fascinated his friend to the point of obsession. "It's a boat, Daniel. If you put a hole in the bottom, it'll sink."

"Are you forgetting the watertight compartments?" Daniel challenged, reaching for one of the many drawings that covered the old editor's table. This one showed *Titanic*'s long hull divided by fifteen transverse bulkheads. "It doesn't matter where the breach is. The captain has only to close the two doors around it to contain the water. Mr. Andrews said she could stay afloat with any four of those compartments flooded."

Paddy shrugged. "It seems simple to me. Flood five."

Daniel shook his head. "It would never happen. A

steamship isn't like a locomotive that can travel sixty miles an hour." He indicated another sketch, this one of the *Titanic* striking a sister ship broadside. "Even a full-speed collision with another vessel would flood only one compartment — perhaps two."

Paddy looked thoughtful. "Maybe your precious *Titanic* isn't the one doing the hitting. What if some other big boat runs into it?"

"*Her*," Daniel corrected. "It would be the same. The other ship's prow would damage one, maybe two compartments, but no more." He looked frustrated. "And there's a double hull. Even if a boiler explodes, it wouldn't break through both of them. A fire on board might do a lot of damage, but it wouldn't burn through heavy-gauge metal."

Paddy put a hand on his friend's shoulder. "If it was easy, your friend Mr. Andrews would have thought of it already. But you're smarter than any starched-up dandy. You'll figure it out. Now, let's go put our bellies around some food. The meat pies should be going onto the sill at O'Dell's just about now."

Not even the promise of a savory meal could wrest Daniel from his sketching. "I'll go later," he said absently. "And remember, don't spend those banknotes."

Paddy cast him a cheeky grin. "Spend? When's the last time you saw me pay for what I eat?"

And he was over the sill and out the window.

It almost didn't count as stealing with Mrs. O'Dell anymore. Ever since Paddy had chased that huge rat out of her larder, she'd looked the other way every time he helped himself to one of her Cornish pasties. If he ever got rich, he would pay Mrs. O'Dell back for every single one he had nicked.

He walked along St. Bart Street, gazing idly into the shop windows and licking his fingers. Daniel didn't know what he was missing. Who would pass up a full stomach to spend the day staring at diagrams of a boat? Sometimes the smart people seemed more stupid than the dullards. But, he reflected with pride, if anybody could come up with a way to sink Thomas Andrews's unsinkable boat, it would be Daniel.

Walking past the window of a stationer's shop, he saw a gorgeous milk-white drawing pad with a complete set of pencils, ink pens, and charcoals of every imaginable thickness. Why, armed with this, Daniel could design a way to scuttle the entire Royal Navy!

A small card beside the display announced that the price of this kit was three crowns sixpence. It was more money than Paddy had ever touched in his life — except for the gold clip he'd taken from the man in the houndstooth cloak. Why, with that windfall, he could afford a dozen of these kits, and have change left over!

He was on the point of running back to where they'd stashed the gold clip when he stopped in his tracks. Daniel had made him promise not to spend any of those banknotes.

But what was the point of having money if you could never spend it? No point at all. And Daniel would forgive him when he saw the wondrous gift he was getting.

Paddy ran to the hiding place and found the stash safe and sound. He plucked a single crisp note out of the clip and knew a moment of temptation. If it was a good thing to purchase this for Daniel, perhaps it made sense to buy each of them a new suit of clothes. If they weren't dressed so shabbily, no one would be suspicious of the money they spent. And they could get closer to a better quality of pocket if they weren't always being chased away as ragamuffins.

No, he decided. *Just buy the kit. Leave the rest of the money here.*

He headed back toward the stationer's.

☆

As morning became afternoon, Daniel began to regret passing up the meat pie. A fellow couldn't very well think on an empty stomach. The lines of his *Titanic* drawings were starting to unravel and dance before his eyes.

It was not going well. Either that, or Mr. Andrews really *had* designed an unsinkable ship.

Daniel reached for a fresh pencil, accidentally scraping his arm against a patch of splintered wood on the old table.

"Ow!"

He examined the damage. An angry red scratch stretched from his wrist to his elbow.

Suddenly, the answer was right in front of him.

He was assuming it would take a spectacular crash to sink a mighty ship like the *Titanic*. But maybe he was approaching the whole problem the wrong way. His skin had barely touched that splintered wood, and yet it had left a wound along the entire length of his forearm. Could the same thing happen to an ocean liner? Not a devastating collision, but a sideswipe that opened a long breach extending through several of her watertight compartments. She could float with damage to four. But what if it was five? Or ten? Or all sixteen?

She would sink, that's what!

He began to sketch with a new energy and excitement.

When he was finished with his diagram, he wrote his name and the date across the top. He couldn't wait to explain his theory to Paddy. Yet the urge to show it to the designer of the *Titanic* himself was almost a physical pain.

He had to get this drawing in front of Thomas Andrews before the shipbuilder's magnificent creation bore him halfway around the world.

CHAPTER FIVE

BELFAST
TUESDAY, APRIL 2, 1912, 4:15 P.M.

The stationer regarded Paddy with suspicion at first, but the freshly printed one-pound note was as good as a letter of introduction from King George himself.

At last, the man said, "I'll be needing to send my boy to the bank with this note, to make sure it's authentic."

Paddy nodded, uncertain whether or not he should be offended. He'd never tried to spend paper money before. Perhaps this was standard practice. He sat awkwardly on a small wooden stool while the stationer wrapped his purchase in butcher paper.

"It won't take long, lad. The bank is just around the corner."

The man was right. It didn't take long. The boy was back within five minutes. Directly behind him was an all-too-familiar man wrapped in a houndstooth cloak.

Paddy's heart turned over. He was caught. Caught! And all because of his own stupidity! Daniel had warned him not to spend those notes!

The stationer addressed the newcomer. "As soon as I saw that quid, I thought this was sure to be one of the little scoundrels you've been looking for."

"It is, indeed," the man confirmed in a gruff voice. "Your help is appreciated, Finn."

"Thank you, Mr. Gilhooley."

Paddy's jaw dropped. "Gilhooley?" Everyone recognized that name. James Gilhooley was the gangster who ran the waterfront district and half of Belfast beyond that.

"I see you've heard of my brother," the newcomer growled. "And now you've met me. The name's Kevin Gilhooley, and you'll not be wanting to forget it."

Paddy could not believe how quickly their good fortune had turned to dust. Just a few days earlier, they had landed a king's ransom, and had been treated as equals by Thomas Andrews himself. Well, when something seemed too good to be true, it usually was. They had stolen from the notorious Gilhooleys. And everyone knew the Gilhooleys never forgave anything. If you sinned against them, you were paid out many times over without exception.

Paddy decided there was no point in trying to lie.

"If we'd known it was you, we never would have done it, Mr. Gilhooley. We'll return your money, every farthing, and you'll not have trouble with us in the future."

"Now, that warms my heart," Kevin Gilhooley replied. "When I look at a thieving little wharf rat like you, I'm reminded of myself as a lad. But you stole from the Gilhooleys, boy, and we can't allow word to get around saying that's an acceptable state of affairs. We have to make an example of you — you and your partner. Now, where would we be finding him?"

Paddy decided, right then and there, that he might have to take his lumps over this, but he would not set these thugs on Daniel.

"We don't need him," Paddy promised. "I'll take you to your money."

Gilhooley's face darkened, and his bushy eyebrows came together to form a single black line. "I was wrong. You're nothing like I used to be. I would have sold out my friend in a heartbeat to save my own skin." In an almost businesslike manner, he removed a brass knuckle-duster from his pocket and slipped it over his right hand. "Take a good look in the pier glass, boy, because you won't recognize yourself when I get through with you."

If Paddy had been the kind to give in to bullies, he would have stayed in the village with his stepfather. But how was he to get away from Gilhooley? The gangster was blocking the doorway.

The man took a menacing step forward.

Paddy jumped up and grabbed the stool he'd been sitting on, brandishing it like a shield.

Gilhooley laughed a cruel laugh. "You'll have to do better than that, boy."

In a split-second decision, Paddy reared back and hurled the stool, not at Gilhooley, but at the shop's front window. The glass shattered into a million pieces, raining down on the pavement outside. Paddy was through that window while the shards were still falling. And once his feet made contact with the cobblestones, he was gone.

He darted around corners, down lanes, and through back gardens, employing all the escape skills he had refined over the past year in order to stay alive. He made at least a dozen turns before even considering starting for home. Daniel had to be warned that they were being hunted by the worst gangsters in Belfast.

He scrambled up the wall to the fire stairs, then squeezed inside the loose board.

A stage whisper: "*Daniel!*" No answer. The abandoned print shop was empty. Daniel had probably gone out in search of food.

Further investigation revealed another detail. All of Daniel's *Titanic* sketches were gone. The surge of excitement almost erased Paddy's fear of the Gilhooleys. Daniel must have taken them to Mr. Andrews! He had solved the puzzle of how to sink the *Titanic*!

But that also meant he was out in the city with no idea that he might be in danger.

Paddy climbed back down to the lane and started at a run for Queen's Island. The streets were crowded, but most people gave him a wide berth. A ragged street boy on the run usually had someone's purse in his possession.

Just outside the entrance to the shipyard, he spied Daniel's slender figure marching along purposefully, the papers rolled up in his hands. Paddy raced to pull alongside him.

"Daniel! Daniel, thank the Lord I've found you!"

Daniel was glowing. "Come with me to see Mr. Andrews! I have the answer!"

"Daniel, listen to me!" Paddy exclaimed. "The twelve pounds in the money clip! We robbed Kevin Gilhooley! That's James Gilhooley's brother!"

"How do you know?" Daniel hissed. "You tried to spend one of the notes, didn't you?"

"Never mind that now!" Paddy pleaded. "They want to use us to show all of Belfast what happens to people who cheat the Gilhooleys!"

Daniel looked thoughtful. "Maybe Mr. Andrews can help us."

"How? He's a shipbuilder, not a copper! And anyway, half the police are on Gilhooley's payroll!"

"He's an important man," Daniel insisted. "If nothing else, we can ask his advice." He turned to the guard at the shipyard gate. "My name is Daniel Sullivan. Mr. Thomas Andrews is expecting me and my friend."

The man checked his list, then regarded Daniel suspiciously. "*You're* Daniel Sullivan? Can you prove it?"

"He knows something important about the *Titanic*," Paddy chimed in. "He's brought sketches to show Mr. Andrews."

The man looked doubtful. "Well, all right," he said finally. "Mr. Andrews is aboard the ship right now, supervising the loading of stores. She's just back from sea trials, and a right lovely job she made of it, too." He smiled. "You can't miss her. She's the big one with the four funnels."

They started toward the wharf. If the *Titanic* dominated Belfast's silhouette, at Harland and Wolff she stood out like a mountain range. The boys needed no directions to find her at her slip. As they made their way through the lineup of delivery wagons, they had to crane their necks to see the top of her mast and towering smokestacks. Yet despite her impressive height, the truly incredible dimension was her length — nearly 900 feet, a full sixth of a mile. Stood on end, she would have almost reached the top of the Eiffel Tower, the tallest man-made structure in the world.

At water level, the main gangway was so much lower than the gleaming upper decks that it seemed more like a pathway under the great ship than an entrance. It was crowded with dockworkers carrying equipment and bales of material aboard. At the bow, a huge hydraulic crane was loading the larger and heavier gear and provisions.

"When are they leaving?" Paddy wondered aloud.

Daniel noted the position of the sun low in the sky. "Soon. We have to find Mr. Andrews right away."

It happened so suddenly that Paddy could barely remember it afterward. Out of the corner of his eye, he caught a glimpse of houndstooth fabric. And then the shillelagh came down across his back, knocking the breath from his body. It was not pain so much as an explosion and an overwhelming force slamming him to the wharf. He heard blows falling elsewhere, and tried to see what was happening. All he could make out through the waves of nausea were several pairs of scrambling legs and big rough boots. Gilhooley's men?

Where's Daniel?

He heard his friend cry out. "Run, Paddy!"

He tried, but his legs were jelly and would not support his weight. He crawled across the weathered planks of the wharf, waiting for the shillelagh's next blow, the one that would kill him.

Running feet pounded across the dock, and a voice yelled, "You take your thuggery elsewhere!"

"Gilhooley's the name!" came the reply. "If you'll mind your own business, my brother and I will be much obliged!"

To Paddy's dismay, the Harland and Wolff employee retreated. He and Daniel were at the mercy of men who had no mercy.

CHAPTER SIX

A large object blocked Paddy's way. He reached for it, and his hand ripped through thick brown paper. Inside was something white and very soft. Sheets and blankets, Irish linens as feathery as clouds. Without even thinking, he rolled over sideways and wriggled his way into the bale, praying to heaven above that no one had seen his escape.

All at once, there was a cry of terror from Daniel, followed by the crack of the shillelagh striking something hard.

Paddy shifted inside his cocoon and peered out to see a dozen papers borne on the wind. One of them slapped against the bale, and he reached out and pulled it in. The four smokestacks jumped out at him immediately. It was one of Daniel's *Titanic* sketches! His friend never would have let go of these unless he couldn't hang on any longer.

Paddy began to struggle madly in an effort to free himself of the tight embrace of the linens. In a part of his mind, he understood that he had no chance of prevailing against a group of brutal Gilhooley gangsters. Yet at that moment, it seemed preferable to emerge and be murdered rather than leave Daniel to die alone.

As he wriggled and thrashed to disengage himself, his body felt a lurch that put his stomach down at his toes. And then the bale of linens lifted from the dock and rose straight up into the air.

He was so totally astonished that, for several terrifying seconds, he was sure that he was being plucked from danger by the hand of God. The reality came to him slowly as the foredeck of the *Titanic* hove into view.

I'm being loaded onto the ship along with the cargo!

But where was Daniel?

He tried to push his head farther out of the bale to gaze beyond the blowing wrapping paper, but it was no use. He couldn't see the wharf. Not unless he wanted to risk falling and splashing his brains all over their brand-new deck.

Frantically, he managed to turn himself around and burrow to the other side of the bale. He punched through the wrapping paper and looked down at the dock. There was no sign of Daniel or Gilhooley's men. The only evidence that they had ever been there was a dark stain on the planking.

Blood.

Daniel's blood.

Even when he'd left his village, his mother, his sisters, and everything he'd ever known, Paddy had not wept the way he now sobbed into the linens that had hidden him and preserved his life.

Daniel was dead. Paddy's fourteen years had been no garden party, but most of his pleasant memories had something to do with Daniel Sullivan. And now his friend was gone, murdered by Kevin Gilhooley and his men.

It never would have happened if I'd listened to Daniel and not tried to spend that banknote. Now he's dead, and it's my fault as surely as if I'd swung the shillelagh myself!

He felt the paper in his hand. The sketch — Daniel's last. He folded it and placed it inside his shirt, next to his heart.

It was peculiar — alone in the world, marked by murderous gangsters, dangling from a crane 30 feet above the deck of a luxury steamship, it wasn't until that moment that the obvious question occurred to Paddy: *What's to become of me?*

One thing was clear: Whatever the White Star Line, or the shipyard guards, or the Belfast police, or even Kevin Gilhooley had in mind for him, it would be no more than he deserved for causing the death of his best friend.

Yet self-preservation was as strong in him as a beating heart. He had not walked halfway across Ireland, had not survived by wits alone in a cruel city, to give up now.

The thump of the linen bundle on *Titanic*'s deck spurred him to action. With a quick look in every direction he could see, he squirmed out of the bale and hit the polished hardwood running. He dashed through an obstacle course of weights and counterweights of various sizes and flattened himself against the housing of a cargo hatch. He peered down and almost lost his purloined meat pie from sheer vertigo. It was at least a 90-foot drop.

Two cast-iron spiral staircases twirled their way to the bottom, exiting at different deck levels. Paddy stepped onto one of them — and froze. He felt rather than heard the footfalls of someone far below climbing up, and retreated to the deserted foredeck.

Beneath the crow's nest, he scampered down a companion stairway to the well deck, and then darted for the immaculate white superstructure. As soon as his worn boots hit the first-class passageway, he was aware of a strange feeling, as if he were running in molasses. It was the carpet — so plush, so thick, that you sank down nearly to the ankles. Paddy had never slept on anything so soft, much less used it just for walking.

The walls — bulkheads — were covered with paneling, freshly painted gleaming white, and dotted with polished brass electric lamps. And, thought Paddy — though he was hardly an expert — the framed pictures looked expensive.

A cabin door stood ajar, and he peeked inside to make sure it was empty. His breath caught in his throat. He had never been to Buckingham Palace, but he could not have imagined that it would be more lavish than this: brass canopy bed, plush velvet draperies, silk wallpaper, vaulted ceiling, delicate furniture, and elegant French doors that opened onto a private promenade deck.

It was hard to believe that the dilapidated, filthy print shop he and Daniel had shared existed on the same planet as this place.

Out the window — a real one, not just a porthole — the buildings and church spires of Belfast stood tall before the surrounding hills. The city had been his home for more than a year. But with Daniel gone, it meant nothing to him. Besides, he couldn't stay there. Gilhooley's men would find him sooner or later. If not tomorrow, then next week, or the week after that.

So here he was, aboard a floating city — and a much nicer version than the one on the other side of the window.

His mind was made up on the spot. On a ship this size, with room for thousands of passengers and crew, who would notice one little stowaway looking for a better life?

He was going to America.

CHAPTER SEVEN

OVER THE ENGLISH CHANNEL
WEDNESDAY, APRIL 3, 1912, 8:20 A.M.

The waves of the Channel glittered in the early morning sun like diamonds.

Not that Juliana Glamm noticed it. At this moment, no subject occupied Juliana's mind other than the safety of the Sopwith aeroplane that carried her and her father a thousand feet above the rocky coastline.

Aeroplane! A glorified kite would be more like it! The biplane was barely more than fabric stretched tightly over a flimsy wooden framework. The slightest puff of breeze sent it reeling. What kept it up in the sky was understood only by a — so far — merciful God.

"She has to be *light*, Julie," her father had explained. "It's all based on the science of aerodynamics."

Juliana held on to her leather seat strap, which was the only thing keeping her tethered to this flying machine. Her father, the seventeenth Earl of Glamford, knew less than nothing about science. His area of expertise tended toward activities that landed him on the society pages — polo, pugilism, gambling, and, now, aviation.

The only part of this flying handkerchief that was remotely substantial was the motor, which was fixed between the double wings, roaring and vibrating, the propeller twirling in front of it. Even this was not particularly reassuring, since the craft was so over-weighted toward the front that a nosedive seemed inevitable. At fifteen years of age, Juliana was far too young to be expected to sacrifice her life just because Papa wanted to be a twentieth-century pioneer.

She craned her neck to look back at her father in the pilot's seat. "When are we going back?" she called over the engine's buzz.

He grinned at her beneath his goggles. "I have a little surprise for you!"

She was wind-battered, terrified, choking on exhaust fumes, nauseated by the bouncing motion, and possibly part deaf from the noise. Her long hair, she was certain, was crushed and limp under her aviator's hood. Who knew how long it would take to brush it out again? This — her first-ever aeroplane ride — was surely surprise enough for today.

But one simply didn't say those things to Rodney, Earl of Glamford. He was a man accustomed to doing as he pleased. Lady Glamm, his long-suffering wife, had given up on trying to cool his passion for gambling and outrageous hobbies. What chance did their fifteen-year-old daughter stand?

She made the mistake of looking down. They were over the rugged coastline now. Gone was the possibility of a soft water landing on the aeroplane's pontoons. If anything went wrong here, they would crash into the chalky gray cliffs.

"Are you sure this is safe?" Juliana asked. "What if the engine stops?"

"As long as there's petrol, the engine doesn't stop," came the reply. Her father took his hand from the stick momentarily to point past the circular shadow made by the whirling propeller. "There, my girl. Take a gander!"

Ahead of them, the dramatic shoreline flattened out, and in the distance, the city of Southampton crept from its bustling seaport onto the English coast.

"What? The town?" The houses looked like matchboxes, the harbor a tiny crisscross of docks.

And then the ship came into focus. At first glance, she looked like just another small boat — until

Juliana realized how far away she was. At least a mile. No, several miles. She counted the smoke-stacks — one . . . two . . . three . . . four.

"Is that —?"

"The RMS *Titanic*, just down from Belfast last night," the earl finished, his grin so wide that it threatened to split his face in two.

In a week's time, Juliana and her father would be a part of the *Titanic*'s maiden voyage, sailing to New York to meet with an associate of Papa's — a man who owned several oil wells in a place called Texas. Gushers, he called them. Such a vulgar word. In truth, the whole thing seemed rather vulgar to Juliana, smelling strongly of the shop. Why would her father rub elbows with a man who drilled holes in the ground, no matter how wealthy he happened to be?

But just as it was futile to predict the patterns of weather that brought, alternately, torrential rain and parching drought to the family's estate outside London, so was it to attempt to understand the mind of the seventeenth Earl of Glamford.

"Isn't she beautiful, Julie?" her father crowed.

That she was. And vast. As the biplane drew nearer, the *Titanic*'s sheer size began to reveal itself. Her immense black hull seemed more like an offshore island than anything man-made. And what an island! Sleek and very long, with a polished deck that shined nearly as bright as the whitecaps, topped by a gleaming superstructure that was, by itself, one of the largest and most modern buildings in the world.

"Shall we go for a closer look?" Her father pushed forward on the yoke, and suddenly, they were falling.

No, not falling — *diving*, the circle formed by the propeller's motion fixed on the *Titanic* far below.

"Papa!" Juliana wheeled around to stare in horror at the pilot's seat behind her. Her father's expression was pure bliss.

Juliana felt her ears pop and pop again as the great ship grew larger and larger. By the time they were within 200 feet of the mast, her astounding length filled Juliana's field of vision. On the poop deck, a terrified dockworker was waving and bellowing.

A common laborer shouting at Rodney Glamm as if the earl were a lunatic escaped from an asylum! Juliana would have been offended — if she hadn't toyed with the thought herself more than once.

And still their wild descent continued.

The earl was in his glory. "What do you say we provide the men with a little entertainment?"

Father and daughter swooped down over the pride of the White Star Line until they were perhaps 50 feet above the top of the *Titanic*'s gigantic smokestacks. Just when Juliana was sure they were about to be dashed to bits, her father pulled back on the stick to bring the aeroplane out of its dive. The craft shook for a moment and then leveled off, taking them directly over the four funnels.

All at once, a deep roar assailed her ears, and a blast of torrid air exploded from the forward stack. Juliana's lungs filled with smoke. She began to cough convulsively. The world around them disappeared, replaced by an acrid black cloud.

But that was not the part that terrified her.

The flying machine dropped, sucked into the downdraft. Frantically, the earl wrestled with the stick in a desperate attempt to pilot the small craft out of harm's way. The biplane heeled over on its side, the double wing passing within a few feet of a catastrophic collision. Juliana saw the enormous smokestack swinging up at her, a giant swatting at a pesky insect. Then, just as suddenly, the pilot regained control, and they climbed out of danger, soaring up and away from the *Titanic* and Southampton.

Even the swashbuckling Earl of Glamford was shaken by the near miss. "Well, that was a bit of excitement, wasn't it, Julie?"

Juliana held on to the seat strap until the thumping

of her heart slowed to the point where she could resume breathing. She peered longingly over her shoulder at the immense bulk of the *Titanic*, dominating the seaport and the English coast.

The rock-solid deck of the largest ocean liner in the world — right now, that seemed like a pretty safe place to Juliana Glamm.

CHAPTER EIGHT

Rich people were mad as March hares.

Of course, Paddy had not met very many wealthy people except to reach into their pockets. But the gymnasium provided for the first-class passengers aboard the *Titanic* was enough to prove that the swells were barmy.

There was a bicycle that was mounted on a stand so the wheels never touched the deck. You could pedal until your legs turned to gruel and not move a single inch.

If I was lucky enough never to have to lift a finger in my life, I wouldn't build some fancy contraption to make me just as tired as everybody else, that's for certain!

He had been sleeping on the exercise mats in the gymnasium's equipment locker for the past four nights — ever since the cargo crane had deposited him aboard the ship. He hadn't planned on being here, but he had to admit it wasn't a bad life. Only a skeleton crew had sailed the *Titanic* down from Belfast, so Paddy had the largest ocean liner in the world pretty much to himself.

Living on the nearly empty *Titanic* was a sight easier than trying to survive on the cruel streets of Belfast. There was plenty of food in the galley, and judging from the size of the cavernous pantries and iceboxes, there was going to be a whole lot more — enough to feed an army. Why, when these shelves were full, even Mrs. O'Dell's meat pies would seem like the meager scraps he and Daniel used to scrounge from dustbins.

Daniel. Just the name was enough to suck the air out of Paddy, and to turn this glittering dream ship into the black dust of the coal that powered her. Daniel was gone, murdered by the Gilhooleys, leaving Paddy with his heartbreak and a string of "if onlys." If only he had chosen a different pocket to pick; if only he hadn't tried to spend that banknote; if only Daniel had been there to talk some sense into him, instead of back in their print shop home, trying to devise a way to sink the *Titanic* for Thomas Andrews.

Paddy felt the drawing beneath his shirt. All he had of Daniel — and all he would ever have. He had examined the diagram, which seemed to show the *Titanic* with a thick jagged stripe down the length of her hull. Paddy wasn't sure how this was supposed to sink the unsinkable. It didn't matter. Daniel was dead. And besides, Mr. Andrews had built the mightiest ship in creation. No accident, no storm, no force of nature could destroy this floating wonderland.

The sheer length of her equaled the distance from their print shop to the River Lagan. The luxury, the modern inventions, would cause the swankiest toff in Belfast to open up wide eyes. The lights ran with real electricity, and there were electric elevators in case you were too rich to walk up the stairs. There was something called a Marconi room, where wireless messages could be sent to other ships and even all the way to shore. There was a heated swimming bath, a squash court, and a Turkish steam room where you could go and sweat — although why anyone would want to do that was beyond Paddy.

For the past few days, he had explored the great ship from prow to stern, making a mental note of every hatch, closet, nook, and cranny that might serve as a hiding place, should the need arise. Everywhere he looked, there was something dazzling. The two grand staircases were massive, solid wood, intricately carved, each topped with a spectacular stained-glass dome. It was like being in church just walking up the stairs. The first-class dining saloon was so huge, so fancy, and so gorgeous, Paddy couldn't imagine anyone being able to think about food. Given a choice, the Pope himself would abandon the Vatican in favor of going back and forth between England and America aboard the *Titanic*.

The experience of being on board was so exhilarating, Paddy would have agreed to live there forever. But he knew the *Titanic* would not remain so empty and free much longer. Already he was noticing more luggage and cargo, and there was definitely an increase of activity on the ship. No longer could he sneak up on deck and peer curiously at England, the country he'd heard so much about but had never dreamed he'd actually see. And even in the vessel's belly, he'd been hearing footsteps and had been forced to take sudden refuge in some of his hiding places. There was no way he could allow himself to be spotted. His ragged clothes would give away the fact that he did not belong in such opulent surroundings.

That was a problem. When the ship was full, he was going to have to be able to fit in. In this way, life aboard the *Titanic* was no different from his old life on the streets of Belfast. What he needed, he had to steal.

The laundry on F Deck was enormous, with dozens of cauldrons that would soon be boiling with soapy water. Paddy looked around. The drying racks were bare, and there was nothing in the hampers. There would be no laundering to do until the passengers and the sailing crew were aboard. He frowned in frustration. Where could a fellow outfit himself in this place?

He was about to leave when he spied a small door in the corner of the compartment. It was not like the wood-paneled entrances in the swankier parts of the ship. This was more like the hatches on the steerage cabins — the lowest class of service on board. He ventured over to investigate. An unfastened padlock hung from the hasp.

Gingerly, he eased the door open and peered inside. The room was filled with crew uniforms, black and bleached white, hanging from a series of racks. He chose a heavy cable-knit sweater bearing the crest of the White Star Line, but abandoned it in favor of a black half coat. Perfect. He'd look a proper sailor in this monkey jacket.

He selected the smallest size — a luxury in itself, that. Beggars had to take whatever castoffs they could find. He peeled off his battered coat and the shirt underneath, which was little more than a rag and smelled none too fresh. He kicked out of his hobnail boots and ruefully noticed his toes poking out of sweaty stockings. His breeches were next — torn, muddy, and too tight. He would not miss those.

As soon as the starched uniform shirt touched his skin, Paddy became aware of a warmth that had nothing to do with the temperature. So this was how rich people felt all the time. Clean, comfortable — a little stiff, perhaps, especially the collar. But it was going to be easy to get used to. He stepped into the trousers and shrugged the black vest and jacket over this gleaming shirt. He caught sight of his reflection in the pier glass and had to fight down the instinct to flee from this stranger in the room.

Lord Almighty, if only Daniel could see me here, looking like the Prince of Wales!

It was a pity to have to step into his tattered boots again, but there were no shoes available. He popped a peaked cap on his head and stuck a bow tie in his pocket. It would probably take him until America to learn how to tie it.

There was a desk at the entrance to the main passageway. Upon it sat a large ledger, pen, and inkwell so the crew members could sign for their uniforms. What a stroke of luck that he'd blundered in here before the clerk came on duty.

No sooner had the thought crossed his mind than the main door opened, and voices reached him from the passageway.

Panicking, he looked around. To make it back to the laundry, he'd have to run out into the open — and his *Titanic* adventure would be over before it began. Desperately, he kicked his discarded clothing underneath the rack and dashed into the changing booth against the bulkhead. He pulled the curtain shut and stepped up onto the stool to keep his boots out of view.

Another way in which life aboard the *Titanic* was similar to Belfast: He was still hiding, still holding his breath, and still praying that he wouldn't be discovered.

☆

"Boy, when I saw you standing on the dock waiting for me, I near jumped off the deck and dashed my brains at your feet!" John Huggins told his son in the uniform room. His voice was deep and scratchy from years of stoking coal in countless boiler rooms.

"I only wish I'd had some better news for you," Alfie said sadly.

The big man ruffled his hair. "Try not to be so hard on your ma. She was never cut out for the kind of life I gave her. She was always lonely, with her head in the clouds. Proper helpless, she was." He bright-ened. "But she surely did right by you. I've got to give her credit for that."

"Right by me!" Alfie exclaimed, outraged. "She shuffled off and left me without a penny to bless myself with!"

"But she made a man of you," his father argued. "The kind of man who had the sense to get hired by White Star so we could sail together. Your old da never would have thought of that. Clever of you, that was."

Alfie was sheepish. "I had to lie about my age. I told them I was sixteen."

"You're not the first, and you won't be the last. Now find a jacket that fits you. You look like you've lost your hands."

Alfie was nervous. "Shouldn't we wait for the clerk?"

"You're not taking anything, just exchanging," John Huggins explained. "It's already signed for. Now I've got to get back to work. She may be the most modern ship ever built, but the boilers won't mind themselves. Imagine that."

Conflicting emotions mingled in Alfie's gut as he watched his father disappear into the passageway. He was happy to be sailing with Da, but the man was practically a stranger. He'd been away at sea for a large part of Alfie's fifteen years. Ma was his real parent — and now *she* was gone. He had no idea if he'd ever lay eyes on her again.

Besides, it wasn't as if the Huggins men would be working side by side. As a fireman, Da would be down in the bowels of the ship, shoveling coal into the *Titanic*'s twenty-nine boilers. As a junior steward assigned to first class, Alfie's duties would keep him many decks above.

"You'll be rubbing elbows with princes and millionaires, boy!" his father had assured him.

It was the talk of the crew. The guest list for the maiden voyage included the very apex of high society: European and British nobility, captains of industry, business tycoons, and wealth that was unimaginable to the likes of Alphonse Huggins. One passenger, a fellow named John Jacob Astor, might have been the richest man in the world. *Might have been!* That was the most astounding part. Not that he was the richest, but the fact that nobody could be sure if he was number one or not. Imagine having so much money that it was impossible to count, so all you could do was guess at how much there was!

Still, Alfie would have gladly traded all of Colonel Astor's vast fortune to have Ma back.

He knew this was a child's way of thinking. He was a man now — at least, he'd told the White Star Line that he was. With a sigh, he began to rustle through the racks of jackets, trying on one that seemed closer to his size. His hands emerged from the sleeves. Yes, this would do.

Back in the passageway, he tried to remember the quickest way back down to Number 5 Boiler Room, where Da would be. By strict rule, Alfie wasn't supposed to be boarding the ship until sailing day, April 10. But he had nowhere else to go, and there were empty hammocks in the firemen's quarters, where his father slept. On a ship the size of the *Titanic*, no one would be the wiser. No one who would report him, anyway. An engine crew was a brotherhood, Da had told him, slaving shoulder to shoulder in the same searing heat, choking on the same steam and smoke and coal dust.

Alfie hesitated. The *Titanic* was a marvel of engineering, but she was also a maze, with dozens of passageways on nine different decks. Da had brought him here via a wide passageway on E Deck that the crew had named "Scotland Road." It was supposed to be the fastest way to get from one end of the ship to the other. But he was on F now. It made no sense that going up could be the most convenient way to get down to the boiler room. Or did it?

As he stood, pondering his route, the door to the uniform room opened and out stepped a very young steward. Alfie was shocked. He'd been positive the compartment had been empty.

A stab of fear. *I admitted lying about my age!*

Spying Alfie, the boy spun around and began marching quickly in the opposite direction.

"Hello," Alfie called tentatively.

The steward broke into a run and disappeared up the companion stairs at the end of the passageway.

Alfie frowned. Had the boy overheard the confession? In truth, the lad seemed even younger than Alfie, but appearances were often deceiving.

Nervously, Alfie reentered the compartment, scanning the racks of uniforms for the steward's hiding place. He noticed the hatch leading to the deserted laundry. Had the boy come from there? Maybe he'd heard nothing at all. . . .

Alfie's eyes fell on a bundle of clothing concealed by a row of trench coats. A jacket, shirt, and trousers, worn and ragged and — he sniffed — plenty pungent, too.

It came to him like the pieces of a jigsaw puzzle

assembling in his brain. The young "steward" — a stowaway? A street boy who had exchanged his rags for a crew uniform in order to pose as a White Star employee?

I must tell an officer at once!

A moment later, rational thought returned. Until April 10, Alfie himself had no business being on board. And if the word got out that he was underage, he would be put off the ship.

Better not to call attention to himself.

What about the old clothes? Should he just leave them here? That would alert everyone to the fact that there was a stowaway.

If the crew began sweeping the entire ship to determine who belonged and who didn't . . .

No, he had to get rid of them. But where? The trash? They'd be noticed there as well.

The image came to mind of the *Titanic's* 15-foot-high boilers, his father and his mates stoking fires hot enough to produce the steam to move the largest ocean liner in the world.

How long could a bundle of rags last in an inferno like that?

CHAPTER NINE

The hustle and bustle on the dock was approaching hysterical proportions. The rush to board more than two thousand passengers and new crew members created nothing less than a mob scene. That was compounded by the relatives and friends who had come to see their loved ones off, and spectators anxious to catch a glimpse of the start of the famous maiden voyage.

The first-class boat train had arrived, and the cream of American and British society poured across the wharf toward the dream ship that would carry them to New York. These titans of the civilized world had to vie for dock space with their own baggage — thousands of crates, steamer trunks, and pieces of hand-tooled leather luggage of every conceivable size and shape. The crane loaded cargo containers that held everything from sacks of mail to a jeweled copy of *The Rubaiyat of Omar Khayyam*, bound for an American museum.

Farther aft, at the third-class gangway, steerage passengers swarmed. Most of them were emigrants, carrying all their earthly belongings in carpetbags and cord-wrapped parcels. White Star officials pored over their identification documents and steamer tickets.

No one bothered first class with such trifles. No sooner had Juliana and her parents stepped aboard than they were whisked to their staterooms by waiting stewards and made as comfortable as the wealthy were accustomed to.

Stateroom B-56 was as sumptuous as any chamber in Glamford Hall, the family's country estate outside London. Juliana could not have been more excited. The suite provided bedrooms for her and her father, as well as accommodations for the maid and the valet. It was a glorious place to be spending the next several days, and she looked forward to the voyage as well as to seeing New York. There was one strangely puzzling development: Why was her mother weeping so?

Elizabeth, Countess of Glamford, clung to her daughter as if she expected never to see her again.

"Please calm down, Mama," Juliana soothed. "It's only a short stay. We'll be home in two months!"

Her reply was only to sob harder. "My darling girl!" she managed.

Her husband, the earl, stepped forward and attempted to embrace her. She whirled away with an expression of deep resentment, and held her daughter once more.

"Your mother is not one for travel," he explained, falsely jovial. "You know how I couldn't coax her into my aeroplane."

"That's because she has an ounce of sense in her head," Juliana teased, trying to lighten the mood. "Would that I had inherited it."

A steward's voice could be heard in the passageway. "All ashore that's going ashore!"

This brought on a fresh bout of weeping.

Juliana would miss her mother, but she was secretly relieved when the Countess of Glamford was escorted off the ship, a steward solicitously holding each arm. She stood, still sobbing, on the dock, waving to her daughter at the rail. It was difficult for a single passenger to stand out aboard the largest ship in the world, but the hysterical countess was making sure everyone noticed her poor daughter.

What could be more embarrassing?

The answer to that came swiftly. A hansom cab

drove up to the edge of the gangway and out stepped two uniformed constables. With perfect gallantry, they helped two ladies alight — one a girl of about Juliana's age, the other a buxom matron dressed, oddly, in purple, white, and green, who had a great deal to say to the policemen, none of it pleasant.

The constables were polite, their decorum never slipping, but their mission was clear: to put these two women aboard the *Titanic* and make sure they stayed.

Sophie Bronson was humiliated. "Mother, if we had arrived with a brass band, we could not possibly have drawn more attention onto ourselves."

The famous Amelia Bronson was unrepentant. "I like attention. It's good for the cause."

"I was hoping," Sophie told her ruefully, "that for this one special voyage, we could forget about the cause. It's already too late for that. Perhaps there's a stoker in the bowels of the engine room who hasn't noticed us being kicked out of England, but everybody else has."

Mrs. Bronson was triumphant in her outrage. "My role is to shed light on the kind of" — she raised her voice so it carried over the bustling dockside — *"injustice visited upon women by an unfair system!* So I'm quite pleased by all this," she finished in her regular voice.

"Begging your pardon, ma'am," said the older of the two constables, "but we're not visiting injustice on anybody. Our orders are just to make sure you're aboard the ship and not to leave until she steams away with you still on her."

Sophie sensed a long, loud reply brewing inside Amelia Bronson's active mind. To stifle it, Sophie picked up a sizable leather bag and set it down firmly on her mother's boot. Seeing a first-class passenger — a lady — actually handling her own luggage brought two porters scurrying over to take charge of their belongings.

A steward followed quickly to take their tickets and escort them to their cabin. "Will your maid be arriving separately?"

"We are women of the twentieth century," Amelia Bronson snapped. "Quite capable of looking after ourselves — and of voting, too, and making other important decisions!"

"Mother . . ." Sophie gritted her teeth and gave her traveling companion a none-too-gentle push.

But the steward was well accustomed to high society and its quirks. "Very good, madam. If you'll be so kind as to follow me." After a few instructions to the porters, he led Sophie and her mother through a dark-paneled foyer, over carpets as thick as the turf of a well-tended golf course.

A real elevator, thought Sophie, hugely impressed. Just like the ones in the skyscrapers of New York and Boston.

Riding up in the car, seeing herself and her mother repeated in the polished brass and mirrors, Sophie was almost sad. This was the experience of a lifetime — the maiden voyage of this masterpiece of modern science and technology. Vast, luxurious, unsinkable — the *Titanic* was all that and more, because she also represented the promise of the wonders to come in this new century.

But Mother saw none of this. She was determined to keep her focus narrow. Suffrage, the cause — that was all that existed for her. It wasn't that she disapproved of the magnificence of the great ship. She simply didn't notice it. The *Titanic* was a means to get home so Amelia Bronson could hold rallies and disturb the peace of American cities, just as she had done in the English ones.

Their suite, B-22, was large and beautifully appointed. Even so, Sophie could not remain indoors. She wanted to be on deck, waving to the crowd. She would not miss this historic occasion. Huge throngs had assembled to see the *Titanic* off, and Sophie intended to be a part of it all. This would be something she could tell her grandchildren. Far better than telling them how she had once spent a night in an English jail in the company of their sainted great-grandmother.

As she stepped out onto the promenade, she was as high up as the steeple of a cathedral. Southampton stretched before her, and beyond that, the deep green of the English countryside.

The horn sounded again — the signal for all ashore. High up, and close to it, the sound was almost deafening. When it died away, it was replaced by the excited chatter of the multitude on the dock, which seemed to have doubled as departure loomed.

Teeming humanity covered every inch of the wharf, except for one spot directly below. An elegantly dressed woman stood there, and those around were giving her a wide berth. She brandished a large white handkerchief, alternately waving it, weeping into it, and then blowing her nose. Even at this distance, Sophie could hear her wailing.

Is she looking at me? Sophie plotted the trajectory of the woman's gaze. *No, not at me, but someone on this deck, just a little farther down . . .*

Sophie's eyes lit on a slender figure, a young girl her own age, perhaps slightly older. Her heart leaped. Another girl! Someone to spend time with, to share the sights and sounds of this amazing voyage. Someone who had never heard of Mother and the cause.

Sophie caught her attention and waved shyly.

The girl's back stiffened. Her reply was not an answering wave, but a curt nod. She turned on her heel and disappeared from the promenade.

Stung, Sophie lowered her hand and her gaze as well. What did she expect? When you arrive at the embarkation point under escort by the police who were expelling you from their country, you can hardly expect to be accepted.

So she was an outcast — and they hadn't even sailed yet.

Thank you, Mother.

CHAPTER TEN

SOUTHAMPTON
WEDNESDAY, APRIL 10, 1912, 12:15 P.M.

Paddy Burns was in pickpockets' heaven.

True, Belfast had been home to purses aplenty, but a fellow had to know what to look for. Here on the *Titanic*'s first-class promenade, the wealth was so abundant, it seemed like you ought to be able to hold out a bucket and have it fill itself with silver and gold.

It was a struggle to keep his eyes in his head as elegant ladies stood waving at the rail, wrapped in thick, lustrous furs and bedecked with jewels that would not have been out of place in the Tower of London. If their menfolk glittered somewhat less, it was in suits and cloaks of such exquisite tailoring that even a Belfast street lad could not fail to notice the quality. Paddy could only imagine the contents of the purses and money clips that bulged beneath all that fine cloth. Far more than the measly one-pound banknote that had cost poor Daniel his life.

The thought triggered a wave of melancholy, and Paddy patted his breast, where he still kept Daniel's sketch for Thomas Andrews.

He had seen Mr. Andrews around the ship several times already. It was strange — for all the *Titanic*'s grandeur, Andrews seemed to see only problems. Paddy had overheard him lamenting the number of screws in the stateroom coat hooks, or the fact that the kitchen stores could accommodate only forty thousand eggs, and not the forty-three thousand the quartermaster had requested. Right now, the great man was on the bridge with Captain Smith and his officers, watching the tugboats guide the *Titanic* to open waters. Paddy couldn't see him, but he imagined the designer's expression — careworn and exhausted from overwork. As if the entire world wasn't singing his praises.

Paddy had considered showing Daniel's sketch to Mr. Andrews. But then Paddy would be revealed as a stowaway. He'd be arrested, locked in the brig until he could be sent to prison in America or England. Of course, there were three square meals in prison, but he'd heard other things about it, too. Terrible things, far worse than an empty belly. It was enough to convince Paddy that he wanted no part of it.

If he could learn Mr. Andrews's stateroom number, he could slip the page under the door. But what earthly good could that do? Paddy had spent hours staring at the drawing. He could not make head or tail of it. Besides, Daniel Sullivan was more than a wrinkled leaf of paper. He was dead, and not even the great Thomas Andrews himself could change that awful fact.

"You there — you're not being paid to daydream!" A white-jacketed steward thrust a tray of brimming crystal champagne glasses into Paddy's hands. "Don't you know who these people are?" he hissed into Paddy's face. "They have to be served before they even think about what they want. Go offer a glass to Major Butt over there. He's military attaché to President Taft. And that's Colonel Roebling. His family built the Brooklyn Bridge, you know. . . ."

The steward listed several other famous names, but none of them meant very much to Paddy, who had never heard of Brooklyn or its bridge. He knew these were fancy people, and very rich — and he also knew that he wasn't here to serve them champagne, or even to walk among them. He'd better get himself out of sight before someone else realized it, too. His uniform made him look like he fit in. But as the voyage progressed, the crew would learn exactly who belonged and who didn't. He was pretty sure he'd spotted that underage steward called Alfie — the one he'd overheard in the uniform room. And if Paddy was recognizing people, other crew members would, too. Possibly even Alfie himself.

Paddy circulated among the passengers at the rail and distributed his drinks in their sparkling glasses. He couldn't prevent himself from smiling. Being so close to so many fat pigeons ripe for plucking made his fingers itch. It was perhaps fortunate that his hands were busy balancing the tray, or he might have come away with enough money to buy legitimate passage aboard this floating palace. Oh, how Daniel would have laughed!

A well-dressed swell, a little younger than the others, put a dove-gray-clad arm around Paddy's shoulders. "You'd best save the last one for Mr. Straus, lad," he said, indicating an elderly man standing with his wife, gazing out over the bow at the tugs. "He's the owner of Macy's department store in New York, you know. They say he's worth more than fifty million American dollars."

Paddy sized the man up. He seemed no different

from any of the other first-class passengers — confident, exquisitely dressed, like he owned the world. Which he probably did, or at least a good chunk of it.

Amazing, Paddy thought dizzily. *A week ago I was eating out of dustbins, and now I'm standing next to a fifty-million-dollar man.*

Suddenly, a series of cracks as loud as gunshots cut through the air. The steel hawsers mooring a smaller ocean liner snapped like wooden toothpicks.

Paddy stared in amazement. It was the American liner *New York* — and it was floating directly into the *Titanic*'s path!

"Are they daft? We'll smash them to bits!"

The young swell peered intently ahead. "That ship isn't moving under her own power."

"Then whose power is moving her?" Paddy asked in alarm. "Are you saying she's sailing herself?"

"The *Titanic* displaces sixty-six thousand tons," the man replied grimly. "The suction must have torn that ship clear out of her moorings. See? She's moving *backward*!"

The festive chatter on the promenade died abruptly as the stern of the *New York* drew closer to the *Titanic*'s port bow, tossing like a dinghy in the over-powering wake of the oncoming liner.

"We're going to ram her!" Paddy breathed.

Hundreds of passengers braced for impact. The fifty-million-dollar man held on to his wife as they watched the drama unfolding below.

The smaller vessel bounced high on a wave and veered around, swinging toward the hurtling black steel of the *Titanic*'s hull.

Paddy closed his eyes, and when he opened them again, it was all over. The *New York* had reeled past them, missing a catastrophic collision by perhaps a few feet.

The swell let out a long breath, and then raised his glass. "To Captain E. J. Smith, the finest, most experienced skipper on the sea!"

Paddy nodded weakly, but in his mind, a discordant note had disturbed the regular thrum of the ship's engines. No amount of experience mattered on board the *Titanic*, which was so much bigger than everything else afloat that she could pull full-size steamers clean out of their secure berths merely by lumbering past. Only *Titanic* experience mattered. And since this was the maiden voyage, no captain had that.

Does anybody really know how to sail this boat? he wondered.

CHAPTER ELEVEN

RMS *TITANIC*
WEDNESDAY, APRIL 10, 1912, 8:45 P.M.

"Papa, if we don't go now, we shall miss dinner."

The Earl of Glamford dismissed his daughter with a fluttering of the two fingers that were not cradling his poker hand. Juliana flinched as her father signed another chit and tossed it in the center of the table. When Papa was embroiled in a card game, the rest of the world simply did not exist.

Another hand, more money into the pot. Juliana was not privy to the Glamms' financial worries, but she would have to have been deaf and dumb not to know they existed. It did not take a chartered accountant to see that her father's fondness for gaming — and his lack of skill at it — was a large part of the problem. She looked around the sumptuous dark paneling of the first-class lounge. The luxurious attention to the tiniest detail was impressive, even to someone reared in a family whose nobility stretched back centuries. Yet all Juliana saw were the card games, poker and bridge, grim-faced players, hand-written markers changing hands in lieu of banknotes.

How can I get Papa out of here?

She leaned close to her father's ear. "Please — it's not proper for me to go to dinner unaccompanied."

"Quite right." Without glancing up, the earl snapped his fingers and a hovering steward came running.

"Yes, sir. May I help you?"

"Kindly accompany Miss Glamm to the dining saloon and see that she is seated. I shall join her shortly."

Face burning with humiliation, Juliana left the lounge on the arm of a steward who was not one hour older than she. Even worse, the young man was very much aware of her discomfort.

"Don't feel bad, miss. When the gentlemen get into the gaming, it's nigh impossible to regain their attention. They wouldn't notice if the ship was sinking."

Juliana was in no mood to be soothed. "This ship is unsinkable," she snapped.

"Well, then, they've got nothing to worry about," he returned softly.

She stared at him in surprise. "You have a lot to say for yourself!"

It was the boy's turn to flush. "Most dreadfully sorry, miss. I didn't mean to be rude."

"And so you weren't," she assured him, ashamed of her ill-tempered behavior. "You were trying to be kind, and I appreciate it."

He was nice but, of course, he was paid to be. Juliana had grown up with servants her whole life. She was fond of some of them, and respected most of them. But their function was no different from that of any other useful item, like a broom or a motorcar.

They descended the magnificent grand staircase, brilliantly lit and dazzling. Other passengers in evening clothes and white gloves, their jewels aglow, passed them on the broad steps, chattering, smiling, relaxed. At Cherbourg, France, more passengers had embarked — most of them wealthy Americans returning from the European social season.

"I'm happy to escort you to your table, miss," the steward told her. "If there might be anything you need, just ask for Alfie, and they'll come and get me." He swept her into the glittering dining saloon.

Juliana had heard that this was the largest single room on any ship ever. She could see now that this description was absolutely true. Drenched with thousands of electric lights and centerpiece candles, fragrant with flowers, and alive with music, the vast space took her breath away. There were so many tables, so many elegant diners — the world's elite, really. How was it possible that Alfie was escorting her to *this* table? Seated there was that girl she had watched board the ship — the one who, along with her mother, had been brought to the *Titanic* by the police.

"Perhaps this is the wrong table?" she asked pointedly.

The problem passed miles above Alfie's understanding. He saw just two young ladies in charming evening gowns. The fact that one was the daughter of an earl and the other was being deported from the country was beyond him.

What could a Glamm possibly have to say to such a person?

Alfie seated her and withdrew. A waiter appeared and draped a snowy linen napkin across her lap.

"You're alone, too," Sophie observed.

Juliana inclined her head. "For the moment. My father, the earl, will be joining me shortly."

"My mother, too. She's in the smoking lounge — puffing on a giant cigar." Sophie noted the other girl's shocked disapproval. "Well, probably not the cigar. But you can bet your last penny she's having a political argument with some men who are growing angrier by the minute. That's the effect Mother has on people."

"Is that why those constables — ?" Juliana blurted. She bit her lip and said no more.

Sophie looked sheepish. "I was hoping nobody noticed that. Your English police aren't sympathetic to votes for women. That's Mother's passion. It means more to her than anything — certainly more than her daughter."

In spite of herself, Juliana experienced a twinge of sympathy. At this moment, she was lower on Papa's list of priorities than a deck of cards. She glanced at the gilded clock. Where was he? He'd promised to follow her in short order. Part of her suspected that he had no intention of coming at all. For Rodney, Earl of Glamford, a poker game was an all-night affair.

"Well, at least you're on your way home now," Juliana offered kindly. "I'm sure your cause is more popular in America."

Sophie sighed. "It's not. The only difference is when Mother is arrested in America, Father is on hand to post her bond." She regarded Juliana curiously. "Is this a pleasure trip for you?"

"I am accompanying my father. He has business in America."

"Oh, what cities will you be visiting?" Sophie asked.

It dawned on Juliana that she had no idea where they would be going, or what the nature of her father's business might be. She knew they were to be met in New York by a Mr. Hardcastle, who owned oil wells. But Papa wasn't in the oil business, was he? Surely not. Papa wasn't in *any* business.

A splendid gentleman who seemed to have gained forty pounds since being measured for his tuxedo arrived at their table. "Bless my soul!" he roared through reddish muttonchop whiskers, seating himself across from the girls. "That I should be so fortunate as to be placed with such an abundance of delightful female company, each one more lovely and charming than the other! I shall become distracted trying to decide which one of you will be first to honor me with the pleasure of a dance!"

The image of being steered around the dance floor backing away from that ample belly nearly caused Juliana to laugh in the gentleman's face. She looked over at Sophie, and saw that the American girl was having the same struggle.

Perhaps the daughter of an earl and an American deportee had something in common after all.

CHAPTER TWELVE

RMS *TITANIC*
Thursday, April 11, 1912, 8:25 a.m.

The heat was unimaginable.

Every time Alfie climbed down the ladder to the orlop deck, he was surprised anew that his memory of it was not half the reality. Twenty-nine boilers 15 feet high, a total of 162 fireboxes, blazes raging. That was what it took to propel the *Titanic*, the largest moving object ever built by man. Added to the temperature was the earsplitting sound of machinery as the steam drove the engines that turned the enormous triple screw that propelled the ship.

It was a crowded place, too. Alfie always had a difficult time locating his father in this roaring hive of activity, the fiery realm of the *Titanic*'s "black gang." It took more than 150 stokers to keep the boilers going, and they all looked alike — shirtless and black from head to toe with coal dust and ash. Da had been working at this on one ship or another for more than twenty years. No wonder his voice sounded like gravel. He must have had a pound of sludge in his lungs.

Another stoker put a grimy hand on Alfie's shoulder and pointed to one of the double-ended furnaces. "Your pa's over there," he rasped.

John Huggins smiled and beckoned. Even here, the closest thing to an inferno Alfie could imagine, his father was always glad to see him. Whatever ill luck that had already happened and might yet befall him, there was that to hang on to. Being loved was no small matter.

"Aren't you on shift, boy?" Alfie's father asked.

"Mrs. Willingham has a shawl that she's especially fond of," Alfie explained. "And I've been sent to the baggage hold to dig it out of her trunk."

John Huggins spat into the roaring firebox. "*Especially fond of!*" he repeated in disgust. "I'm sure she's got seventeen more in her stateroom. It's a blessing to be working class. Money makes you soft in the head."

Alfie laughed. "Then I must have the hardest head of anybody. They're paying me three pounds ten for the entire voyage."

His father jammed his shovel into the bin and came away with a scoopful of smoldering, smoking coal.

Alfie was alarmed. "Your bin is on fire!"

"Easy, lad," his father soothed. "That happens when you're working with coal. You're supposed to keep it well watered, but some of the younger blokes just wet the top of the pile and don't worry about what's down below."

"But fire at sea?" Alfie persisted.

"That's not fire, lad." He indicated the relentless flames inside the furnace. "*That's* fire. Now, you'd best be off. Can't keep a rich lady waiting for her favorite wrap."

Alfie left his father and continued on his errand, passing through Number 6 Boiler Room. As he ducked through the hatch, he imagined the heavy watertight door that would clatter down at the flip of a switch by Captain Smith. Down here, it was easy to visualize the sixteen sealed compartments that made the ship unsinkable.

A delicious coolness washed over him as he entered the fireman's passage forward of Number 6. A thermometer on the bulkhead read 88 degrees, but the improvement was measureless.

It took all his strength to open the heavy iron hatch to his left. Trunks, boxes, and luggage were piled nearly to the ceiling, secured in place by thick netting — the worldly goods of more than six hundred first- and second-class passengers. It would surely take half the night to find Mrs. Willingham's belongings. And by then, some other fancy-pants would no doubt send him on his next mission — after a watch fob or a makeup mirror this time.

He yanked open the hatch to his right, hoping against hope to see Mrs. Willingham's trunk standing alone and unsecured, awaiting his key. No such luck. There was, instead, a vast cargo hold. Crates of all sizes, containing everything from tea to machine parts, were stacked one on top of the other, tightly tied down.

As if a wave exists large enough to toss a ship this size, thought Alfie. The *Titanic* rode the Atlantic so sturdily that a pencil could be stood upright on a tabletop. He had seen it several times. It was a favorite game in the first-class lounge.

He surveyed the hold, his gaze passing over bales of rubber, rolls of linoleum, sacks of potatoes, and barrels of mercury and the scarlet resin called dragon's blood. In the center of the compartment was parked a motorcar! It was large and bright red, yet it was almost completely hidden by the endless cases and parcels and casks.

And then something inside the automobile *moved*!

CHAPTER THIRTEEN

Alfie froze. "Is someone there?" he asked in a high-pitched voice.

There was no answer and no more movement. He had a small argument with himself. Was it part of a junior steward's duties, for less than four pounds, to see if anyone was hiding in there?

Good sense told him no, but curiosity won the day. He picked his way through the piles of cargo and gingerly approached the motorcar. As he peered in through the windscreen, the last thing he expected to see was a pair of eyes looking back at him.

Twin gasps of shock rose in the hold.

With surprising speed, a small wiry figure in a rumpled steward's uniform leaped out of the automobile, sending a stack of hosiery cases toppling. He stood, poised, as if trying to decide whether he should fight or flee. Hemmed in by piles of cargo, escape seemed unlikely, and a struggle might bring half the crew down upon them.

Alfie stared at him. "You're the one I saw in the uniform room!"

"So I was sleeping on the job," Paddy blustered. "So what?"

"You don't work here!" Alfie exclaimed. "You're a stowaway! I saw the rags you threw off!"

"You must be thinking of someone else, friend," Paddy insisted through clenched teeth.

"Perhaps we should let the captain make that decision. There's a telephone to the bridge just outside in the fireman's passage."

"You do what you think you have to," Paddy replied grimly. "And while he's here, we can also ask him why a lad of fifteen is signed on to his crew."

Alfie winced. "How do you know that?"

"I might have overheard a little father-and-son chat in that same uniform room," Paddy told him with a slight smile.

"You're a stowaway," Alfie accused again.

"That I am," Paddy admitted. "And you're underage. So we'll have each other for company when we're put ashore at Queenstown before the *Titanic* crosses to America."

"I think sneaking aboard a steamer bound for New York is more serious than a wee exaggeration in the hiring line," the young steward said, a little less certainly.

"Looks like we're going to find out, then." Paddy sensed his advantage and pressed it. "I feel sorry for you, I do."

"For *me*?" Alfie challenged.

"Well, if I get the bum's rush, I'm right about where I started. But you've got a job — and your pa . . ."

"I won't tell anybody about you," Alfie blurted quickly.

"Now, where would the justice be in that?" Paddy began to pick his way through the maze of cargo. "Perhaps I'll telephone the bridge myself —"

"Please don't," Alfie pleaded.

But Paddy did not stop. "All this is weighing on my conscience something terrible. And it wouldn't hurt to put some food in my belly. Even in the brig, there's a square meal to be had."

"I'll bring you food!"

The stowaway turned around and favored Alfie with a grin. "A sandwich would be lovely. And a glass of that nice, rich milk."

Light dawned on Alfie. "You blackmailing little gangster!"

Paddy's expression darkened suddenly. "A black-mailer I may be, but you'll not call me a gangster. . . ."

Alfie took a nervous step back, even though he was a head taller than the other boy. "I —"

"Gangsters murdered my friend," seethed Paddy, his eyes glazing over. "Do you think I'd be aboard this ship if Daniel was still alive?"

"I'm sorry," stammered the young steward. "I'll bring you food. But first I have to find Mrs. Willingham's favorite shawl!"

Paddy stared at him for a moment and then burst out laughing. "Well, we can't deprive a rich lady of that, can we? Any search this important demands two pairs of eyes!"

He followed Alfie out of the cargo hold, through the fireman's passage, and into the baggage compartment. "I've been in here before," he commented casually. "Everything's locked."

Alfie turned on him sharply. "There'll be no stealing or our deal is off!"

"Don't get your knickers in a twist," Paddy chuckled. "Why would I need to steal if someone's bringing me food?"

"I want your word on it!"

"Like you gave yours to the White Star Line?" Paddy returned.

They began to scan luggage tags, which identified each trunk and crate according to the owner's deck level and cabin number.

"Look at this!" Paddy held up a leather-bound book thick with inserts.

The young steward was angry. "Put that back!"

"I didn't take it," Paddy defended himself. "It was just lying here on the deck. It must have fallen out of one of the trunks. I wonder what it is."

"It's none of your business, that's what it is!"

"There's no name on it." Paddy set the volume on top of a large box and opened it to the first weathered page. "It seems to be some kind of scrapbook." A newspaper broadsheet was carefully pasted there. The headline read:

GHASTLY MURDER IN THE EAST END

Paddy stumbled over the first word, but the second he recognized at once. "Murder!"

It brought Alfie swiftly to his side. "What murder?"

Paddy indicated the newspaper. "Read it for yourself! Some lady in London was murdered with a knife! There was blood everywhere! It's horrible!"

"This newspaper is old," Alfie pointed out. "Look

how yellow it is. And the date — September second, eighteen-eighty-eight, twenty-four years ago. Mary Ann Nichols — why does that name sound familiar?"

"It can't," Paddy concluded. "She was dead before you were born."

Alfie leafed through the scrapbook. There were newspaper stories of dreadful killings on every page, along with maps of London and line drawings of gruesome crime scenes. "These are the Whitechapel murders!"

"What-chapel?"

"Whitechapel — it's a part of London!" Alfie explained breathlessly. "The whole of England lived in fear for months! People were afraid to leave their flats and houses. When I was a wee lad, my ma used to say, 'Alfie, I won't sleep sound in my bed at night until that monster is off the street for good.' Even now, after twenty-four years, they've never found the killer! Ma's still obsessed with the subject."

"So is one of the passengers," Paddy said. "What sort of person makes a pastime of recording the foul deeds of a terrible criminal?"

"This is no pastime," Alfie countered, his face paling as he scanned the pages. "Look at this!" He pointed to a note scribbled by hand in the margin beside an account of one of the murders: *Hanbury St. — extinguished gaslights 3 & 4.* "No mere scrapbook keeper could know details like these!"

A small cloth envelope was fastened to the cardboard beneath the broadsheet. With a none-too-steady hand, Alfie unfastened it and tapped the contents into his palm. Out tumbled a large, garish jade earring and two tiny objects, lumpy and ivory-colored. His eyes widened in revulsion.

"Teeth!" Paddy hissed. "Human teeth!"

Alfie jerked his hand away as if he'd been burned. The three items dropped to the deck of the hold. The earring lay there, but the teeth bounced and skittered, disappearing among the piled trunks and baggage.

"Trophies!" Alfie rasped in horror. "Souvenirs of the people he's butchered!"

"Are you saying there's a murderer aboard the *Titanic*?" Paddy asked in amazement. "Who could it be?"

"The Whitechapel murderer was never identified," Alfie replied, his voice filled with dread, "but his nickname is well known across England." He let out a tremulous breath. "Jack the Ripper."

CHAPTER FOURTEEN

PORT OF CALL: QUEENSTOWN
Thursday, April 11, 1912, 11:35 a.m.

Ireland.

Now that he had Alfie sneaking him food, Paddy resolved to pass the voyage in hiding. But he couldn't resist the chance to come up to the second-class promenade and take in the sight of the land of his birth.

How beautiful it looks!

In truth, it was not very beautiful. A misting rain and low overcast sky washed its green into a wet, dirty gray. And anyway, Queenstown was hundreds of miles away from Paddy's village in County Antrim. To an Ulster boy, Cork, the southernmost county, might as well have been in England or even America.

So how did he explain the empty space where his heart was supposed to be? Why were his eyes filled with a moisture that had nothing to do with the rain? Why did this alien place feel like home?

Like Cherbourg, Queenstown's harbor was too shallow for a large ocean liner. Paddy squinted at the mass of passengers packed aboard the tender that chugged slowly toward the anchored *Titanic*. Even from this distance he could make out the worn cloth coats and caps, the carpetbags in drab beiges and browns. Alfie had told him that no first-class passengers would be boarding at Queenstown, and only a handful of second class. The rest of the group — more than a hundred strong — was steerage.

Maybe that was why Queenstown seemed so familiar. These were poor people.

Like me.

He felt an almost irresistible urge to get off this floating palace. The impulse made no sense. Ireland meant poverty and hunger, having to steal to survive. How could he choose that over a dream ship filled with millionaires and equipped with luxuries he'd never even known existed?

Maybe that was the problem. The *Titanic* was too big, too rich, too perfect. There was something wrong with that. It wasn't real. He'd been wrestling with the uneasy feeling ever since Southampton, when the enormous ship had sucked the *New York* into a near collision.

Now, seeing Ireland within reach again, the solution suddenly seemed simple. If he could stow away aboard the mighty *Titanic*, he could surely sneak onto the little tender that was bringing out the last contingent of passengers.

He was Irish. Ireland was where he belonged. When the small ferry unloaded its human cargo and went back to Queenstown, Paddy Burns intended to be on it.

His feet began to move almost of their own accord. He was being carried toward home by a force he could no longer resist. Before he knew it, he was stepping onto the elevator to E Deck, where the new passengers would be coming aboard.

"I don't think I've seen you before," the lift operator commented pleasantly.

"And you'll not be seeing me again," Paddy replied. It no longer mattered if he was identified as an imposter. What could they do? Put him off the ship? He was putting himself off.

"Good luck to you, then. A word of advice. If you're really leaving us, you'd best change out of the uniform or they'll hound you to the ends of the earth."

Paddy laughed. "They can try."

If Alfie Huggins was an example of White Star material, Paddy had nothing to worry about. The young steward seemed a nice fellow, but it hadn't been very hard to blackmail him into protecting a stowaway. A few months in the neighborhoods of Belfast provided more education than all the schools in England.

Poor Alfie wouldn't have lasted ten seconds on Victoria Street. He was too absorbed in a series of crimes from twenty-four years ago to worry about what might be coming around the corner to clobber him right now. Jack the Ripper aboard the *Titanic*! What next?

Paddy navigated the E Deck passageway and reached the gangway just as the tender was tying up. He already had all his worldly possessions — the suit on his back and Daniel's drawing. Too bad he couldn't have managed a few fat purses from first class. That would have kept him in meat pies for a long time. But he couldn't risk missing the tender.

His plan was simple: He would pose as a White Star employee escorting the Queenstown passengers ashore, and he would simply never come back.

He melted into the group as the gate was lowered and the stewards began welcoming the new arrivals.

He saw the bodyguard first — a very tall, rough-looking man with impossibly broad shoulders and a broken nose that wandered all over his face. Next, the houndstooth cloak appeared, and above that, cold, cruel eyes deep set in a stone countenance.

The blood drained from Paddy's body and settled in his trembling feet.

Kevin Gilhooley, the man who had killed Daniel.

The man who wanted Paddy dead.

The irony was shattering. To escape this monster, Paddy had sailed from Belfast to Southampton to Cherbourg to here. Yet all this time, Kevin Gilhooley had been traveling by rail across Ireland to embark on the very same ship.

The man's eyes locked on him, and widened in surprise and recognition.

In that instant, the *Titanic* disappeared, and Paddy was back on the streets of Belfast, where the only thing that mattered was staying alive.

He fled. Through passageways, anterooms, and salons he dashed, up and down companion stairs, past unadorned iron hatches and opulent entrances. Behind him, he felt the pursuit in the form of heavy, pounding footfalls. But he also heard it — shouted instructions between Gilhooley and his henchman.

"He went that way!"

"Don't let him get away!"

How can the Titanic's *reception party allow two thugs to run rampant all over the ship, threatening a crew member, even an imposter?* he wondered as he ran. The answer was obvious. Stewards were trained to cater to the whims of millionaires and the fears of hopeful emigrants. That sort of treatment did not work well with a gangster like Gilhooley. His ilk did as they pleased. And if someone stopped them, it was usually someone even bigger, stronger, and meaner.

Paddy hustled through the third-class dining saloon, rows of long tables, the decor pleasant but spare and severe. The passageway continued for a distance, ending at a half-gate, used aboard ship to divide classes of service.

Paddy leaped over it without stopping. As soon as his feet touched down, he was aware of the plush carpeting. The paneled walls and subtle lighting told the rest of the story. This part of the deck saw first-class traffic.

The swimming pool, Paddy remembered. *It's around here somewhere.*

He slipped through an elegant door marked TURKISH BATH and was amazed to find himself in a gorgeous room that looked like an Arabian palace. Lounge chairs lined the dark walls, and a few men reclined, wrapped in huge thirsty towels. Two of them even had towels over their faces. It was a scene of total pampering and relaxation, the kind only a true swell could afford.

The attendant acknowledged Paddy with a nod, and then stepped into the adjoining steam room.

Gruff, angry voices sounded in the passageway outside. His pursuers were almost upon him!

Paddy did the first desperate thing that came to his mind. He jumped onto the nearest unoccupied lounge chair, buried himself from head to toe in warm Turkish towels, and prayed that the attendant hadn't counted his customers when he'd gone next door.

A moment later, the hatch burst open and Gilhooley and his man stormed into the bath.

"He's not in here!" the bodyguard growled. "This is some kind of posh bathhouse!"

"The devil he's not!" Gilhooley roared. He grabbed at the nearest wrapped figure and yanked the towel clean off.

"How dare you, sir?" came an outraged, authoritative voice.

At that moment, the attendant came back into the room and took in the scene. "Please, sir! Don't you know who this is? It's Colonel Astor! He's not to be disturbed, nor is anyone in my care!"

"There's a thief on board!" the bodyguard growled. "We followed him to this part of the ship."

"You are mistaken, I'm sure," the attendant said stiffly. "This part of the ship is for *gentlemen*." The word clearly excluded them. "If you do not leave at once, I shall have to call the master-at-arms."

The henchman pulled himself up to a full six feet and four inches. "You do what you must. I can break two necks if necessary."

Gilhooley held him back. "Easy, Seamus. This is a ship. The little rat has nowhere to run. We'll find him soon enough. And when we do, he's going over the side."

Paddy lay beneath the towels, barely daring to breathe.

As Gilhooley and his man left, Paddy heard the voice of John Jacob Astor once again. "Well done, Joseph," the wealthiest of the wealthy praised the attendant. "I shall mention your handling of this situation when I dine with the captain this evening."

Amen, thought Paddy. But now he faced another problem. The Turkish bath that had saved him was now his prison. He couldn't very well leave without being noticed. Yet it was more important than ever for him to get off the ship at this last port. Once they headed into open ocean, there would be no escape. He would be trapped on board with two Gilhooley gangsters. And then surely he would never see New York.

He needn't have worried. After a few minutes, a voice in his ear whispered, "Come with me — not a sound."

Paddy got out from under the towels. Colonel Astor and the other gentlemen were either covered up or dozing. He followed Joseph through the steam room and onto the deck of the swimming bath.

"I'm not going to ask what you took from those brutes," the attendant told him in a low voice.

Twelve pounds, Paddy thought dismally. Would that he'd never reached his hand inside that cloak! Aloud, he said, "A long, sad story, it is."

Joseph did not press him further. "Stay clear of those two," he advised before returning to his very important customers. "They look more than capable of turning their threats into reality."

Paddy made no reply. All his attention was focused on the porthole closest to him. It showed the departed tender halfway back to Queenstown Harbor.

He was too late.

CHAPTER FIFTEEN

PORT OF CALL: QUEENSTOWN
THURSDAY, APRIL 11, 1912, 1:30 P.M.

Captain E. J. Smith, Commodore of the White Star Line, the finest and most experienced master of any ship on the high seas, stood ramrod straight on the bridge of the *Titanic*. His eyes were not on Queenstown, but on the open Atlantic. That was the style that had made him a legend — focus exclusively on the path ahead. It made no difference where one had been, only where one was going.

The ocean was reassuringly calm, as if in tribute to his final crossing. Captain Smith was retiring after taking the *Titanic* on her maiden voyage. It was fitting that his last command would be a memorable one.

"All right, Mr. Lightoller," he addressed his second officer. "Weigh anchor."

Suddenly, a very young seaman rushed onto

the bridge, all agitation. "Sorry, sir! I tried to stop them —"

Kevin Gilhooley and his huge henchman, Seamus, elbowed their way into the captain's presence.

"Captain, you have a criminal among your crew!" Gilhooley accused.

"What I have," Smith said sternly, "are two passengers who have not been invited onto the bridge."

"I told them, sir! They wouldn't listen —"

"At ease, Mr. Loomis," said the captain, always under perfect control.

Kevin Gilhooley was not accustomed to having his requests ignored. "Did you not hear me, Captain? I said one of your crew is a thief! I saw the boy not half an hour ago! I demand that you assemble the contingent and allow me to identify him."

The captain grimaced. "*I* do the demanding on this vessel, sir."

Standing behind Mr. Lightoller, Thomas Andrews, designer of the *Titanic*, spoke up for the first time. "Allow me to make the introductions, Captain. I live in Belfast, so I'm familiar with this man's family. They are involved in a number of activities that are — shall we say — frowned upon by the authorities."

Smith nodded his understanding and turned back to Gilhooley. "You may feel free to pursue legal remedies with the police in New York. But aboard this ship, *I* am the law. If that is unacceptable to you, my officers can arrange to have you put ashore here in Queenstown. I trust that's clear."

Gilhooley was livid. "You're protecting a criminal! The White Star Line will hear about this!"

A shorter man with a prominent handlebar mustache stepped forward. "The White Star Line has already heard. I am J. Bruce Ismay, the managing director. How do you do?"

Gilhooley grew even redder. "You stuffed shirts always line up against the common man!"

"Indeed we do," agreed the captain cordially. "Now kindly vacate my bridge. I'm sure you have some unpacking to do. Mr. Loomis will see you to your cabins."

When Gilhooley and his man were gone, Second Officer Lightoller spoke up. "Standing by to weigh anchor, sir."

"I gave that order, Mr. Lightoller."

"Captain, the quartermaster informs me that we have only enough binoculars for the bridge crew, not for the lookouts in the crow's nest. Shall I send ashore for additional glasses?"

Before the captain could reply, Mr. Ismay offered his opinion. "Of course, I'm merely a passenger, but we're already behind schedule because of that unfortunate incident with the *New York*. Do we really want to suffer any additional delay?"

"Quite right," decided the captain. "A true seaman sees better with the naked eye. Take us out, Mr. Lightoller."

Minutes later, the great ship began to move toward open ocean.

Captain Smith savored the thrum of the *Titanic*'s huge reciprocating engines rising from the deck beneath his feet.

One last voyage.

CHAPTER SIXTEEN

RMS *TITANIC*
THURSDAY, APRIL 11, 1912, 3:45 P.M.

The view from the boat deck was like nothing Sophie had ever seen. Here, eight stories above the Atlantic, she was surrounded by endless sea and cloudless blue sky. It was so clear that she could actually make out the curve of the earth at the horizon.

She lay back in her deck chair while Alfie tucked a warm woolen blanket around her. "It's cold out here, miss. I brought you a mug of hot bouillon. We can't have you taking a chill."

"What is it about bouillon on this boat?" Sophie complained. "The wealthiest people on earth wouldn't feed it to their dogs anywhere else. But here they swill it like it was the finest champagne!"

Alfie was taken aback. "I can get you tea or chocolate if you prefer."

She laughed mirthlessly. "Pay no attention to me, Alfie. I'm having a terrible voyage."

"But why, miss?" Alfie enquired. "You're aboard the finest ship in the world."

In answer, Sophie gestured over the rail to A Deck below them. The windows in the first-class lounge were open, and strident voices could be heard in a strenuous argument. There were several men trumpeting with outrage. But the loudest of all was decidedly female.

"Women are only irrational because the standards of rationality have been established by men!" Amelia Bronson held forth. "You've been in charge since the dawn of history, and what do we have to show for it? War! Hunger! Slavery! We should *all* choose our leaders, not merely half of us. Then you'd see a revolution without bullets or bloodshed!"

"Madam!" came an indignant bluster. "I never thought I'd say this to a lady, but you are *no lady*!"

"Agreed!" Sophie's mother roared. "I am a human being, just as you are!"

"I suppose you can hear that." Sophie sighed miserably. "They can probably hear it back in England."

"I'm told that she's also trying to organize the women on board," Alfie said sympathetically. "Perhaps first class isn't the right group for it."

"Don't tell her that!" Sophie exclaimed quickly.

"She'll go to second class and start recruiting there. And then steerage. We'll be put in a lifeboat and set adrift in the middle of the Atlantic!"

"No one thinks of lifeboats on an unsinkable ship, miss." Alfie chuckled. "Aboard the *Titanic*, they either hang you from the yardarm or make you walk the plank. Cheer up. Here comes Miss Glamm to keep you company."

In fact, the girl was practically running, holding on to her long skirt as she hurried up the companion stairs. She rushed over and sat down in the chaise next to Sophie's, sinking low.

"A blanket, Alfie. Quickly!"

"I can fetch more bouillon if you're cold," the young steward offered.

As he tucked a blanket around her, she pulled it right up to her nose. "I'm not cold; I'm *hiding*. Major Muttonchop is about! He wants to finish his story about tiger-hunting in India!"

Sophie groaned. "He is, bar none, the most boring man on the face of the earth. You have no idea how much I was pulling for the tigers. How could you lead him to me, Julie?"

Juliana laughed. "I think I gave him the slip on the Grand Staircase."

"Oh, you mean Major Mountjoy, the gentleman from your dining table," Alfie put in. "Belowdecks they call him Old Windbag. He does go on and on."

Juliana cast him a look of stern disapproval. "I'm certain that the White Star Line forbids you to gossip about your betters."

Alfie stared at her as if she had just slapped him. "But you just said —"

Sophie tried to come to his rescue. "This is Alfie's first voyage as a steward. He didn't mean any harm."

"I'm certain he did not." Juliana was gracious but unforgiving. She rose from her chair. "Perhaps I had best find Papa." And she was gone in a swirl of skirts.

"You have to understand, Alfie," Sophie tried to explain. "She's not a bad person, but she was raised in a house filled with servants who were no more to her than pieces of furniture. That's the only life she knows."

Alfie was chagrined. "It's I who should apologize. I chased your friend away. I'm most dreadfully sorry."

Sophie passed this off with a wave of her hand. "I don't want conversation. I don't want to read a book. I just wish something would *happen*."

Alfie blinked. "We're on a ship in the midst of an ocean crossing, miss. What could possibly happen?"

"Something that would take my mind off the fact that my mother is picking fights with the most important people alive." She scowled. "And what that might be, I have absolutely no idea."

Alfie raised an eyebrow. "What if I told you there's something on this ship that would turn your mind upside down and inside out?"

"What?" asked Sophie, intrigued.

"I can't explain. I have to show you. Tonight."

☆

Sophie spent the rest of the afternoon checking the progress of the sun as it sank toward the horizon off the bow.

Finally — something to look forward to besides Mother being strung up by a mob of angry millionaires.

Her thoughts crackled with speculation. What could Alfie be on about? What was this mysterious object that would turn her mind "upside down and inside out"? She hoped with all her heart that it would not turn out to be just another porthole with a slightly different view of the interminable waves. Sailors thought there was nothing more fascinating than the sea. But stewards weren't sailors, were they? Especially a steward on his very first crossing.

This *had* to be something good.

At the same time, her anticipation was tempered by a little nervousness. Had she really agreed to meet a boy at eleven o'clock at night for some unknown adventure? Was that wise, or even sensible? Why, twenty years ago, a young lady caught alone with a man would be expected to marry him! Then again, twenty years ago someone like Mother could be hanged for sedition. At minimum, when the constables threw her in prison, they wouldn't let her out again a few days later to catch a first-class boat.

Sophie relaxed a little. That was Juliana's world, the world of a previous century. This was 1912. Mankind had advanced to a point where light and heat came from wires carrying electricity, and Mr. Thomas Andrews could design an ocean liner that was unsinkable. Things *were* changing — even if it wasn't quickly enough for Mother.

She stayed on the boat deck as long as she could bear it, and then started to her cabin early to dress for dinner.

As she walked along the passageway on B Deck, a soft juicy snort reached her ears. She rounded the corner and nearly tripped over him — a slender well-dressed gentleman sitting crumpled against the paneled bulkhead, smelling of stale tobacco and brandy. Even fast asleep and snoring, there was an elegance to the man in the way his tall frame folded neatly into the corner between the brass rail and the carpeted deck.

If Mother were here, the speech would be loud and long: *They entrust this drunkard with the vote while millions of informed, intelligent women . . .*

Recognition came as almost a blow. This was no ordinary drunkard. This was the Earl of Glamford, Juliana's father!

Sophie had been about to send for a steward, but how could she do that now? If there was one thing the first-class passengers liked more than money, it was gossip. The story of the English nobleman who had to be scraped off the deck and poured into his cabin would make its way back and forth across the Atlantic for years. Juliana would die of humiliation.

Her mind made up, Sophie reached down and shook the sleeping man by the shoulders.

"Your lordship," she whispered. "It's Sophie Bronson, Julie's friend."

The earl gave no answer, but a large bloodshot eye opened and looked at her in confusion.

"You're on B Deck," she tried to answer his unspoken question. "Not just that part of the ship — on the deck itself. The *floor*. Do get up, and I'll help you to your suite."

When he made no move to stand, she hauled him to his feet, inserted her shoulder under his arm, and half carried him down the passageway to stateroom B-56. It was a struggle. He was an athletic man, and no lightweight. Mother would have been impressed. A woman carrying a man. Weaker sex? Fie!

At last, wilting under her burden, she managed to scratch at the door.

Juliana's maid, Elsie, took in the sight of her employer and gave a little shriek.

Juliana appeared behind her. "Sophie?" Her eyes fell on the spectacle of her father.

The three young women managed to walk him to his bed. When they stepped back from him, he dropped like a stone and lay unmoving. The snoring resumed.

"It's the cards," Juliana explained sadly. "He drinks when he plays, especially when he's losing."

"I didn't know what to do," Sophie confessed, catching her breath. "I didn't think you'd want me to call the stewards."

Juliana nodded gratefully. "You're a real friend. I am in your debt. Any time I can do you a service, you have but to say the words."

Suddenly, Sophie knew exactly what she was going to ask for.

CHAPTER SEVENTEEN

RMS *TITANIC*
THURSDAY, APRIL 11, 1912, 11:10 P.M.

It was dark on the spiral staircase that led down the Number 2 Hatch. The space was so cavernous that Alfie's kerosene lantern cast only a dim glow around the three figures. Juliana could barely see the hem of the gown she'd worn to dinner. It was hours later now, and the ship had grown quiet. The music and dancing had ended some time earlier, and the passengers had retired to their staterooms, or their cigars, or their card games.

Cards. For once, Juliana wasn't worried about her father's poker losses. Papa had declined food, and was stretched out on his bed. He had been asleep since before the bugler had summoned first class to dinner. He was going to have a paralyzing headache when he woke up. With any luck, that would be long after this late-night escapade was over and his daughter was back in their suite again.

Have I gone mad? she wondered.

What was she doing skulking around the bowels of the *Titanic* with an untamed American girl and the steward she had inexplicably decided to befriend? But after promising Sophie a service, how could she refuse?

So here she was, in the working part of the ship, where it was not seemly for passengers to visit. Surely not the behavior expected of a Glamm. Mind you, the head of the family hadn't exactly distinguished himself today. So any disgrace Juliana might bring down on them could only be second to his performance. Whatever happened, she was in for a penny, in for a pound — or those American dollars everyone was so keen on.

"Now, if we run into anyone," Alfie said in a low voice, "remember what I told you. I'm your steward escorting you to your luggage to get something you need."

"I don't see why we have to go down to the hold ourselves," Juliana complained. "Why couldn't you have brought this item up to us?"

"You'll see, miss," Alfie promised. "This isn't the kind of thing that you can flash around."

"Is it just me or is it getting warmer?" Sophie put in nervously.

"The boiler rooms are just aft of us," Alfie explained. "Don't worry; we won't get too close to them. I've been there to visit my da on the black gang. You feel like the air you breathe is on fire in your lungs."

"Alfie." Sophie's voice was subdued. "If we get caught here, Julie and I will be scolded. But what will happen to you?"

"I can't really say," he replied, so readily that it was obvious the thought had been haunting him. "I suppose it would depend on who catches us. But this discovery I've made has been bubbling up inside of me. I'll burst if I don't share it."

Juliana knew all too well what would happen to Alfie if they were caught. He would be relieved of duty and placed under arrest for the remainder of the voyage. He might even be stranded in New York. Employees dismissed for cause could expect no better. His father's pay might purchase him third-class passage back to England on a different ship. But he would never set foot aboard the *Titanic* again. What could he possibly have to show them that was worth such a fate?

They descended the metal staircase more than 70 feet into the depths of the ship, well below the waterline. It was a disconcerting thought to both girls that the surface of the ocean was actually *above* them. Yet, apart from the heat, the air felt no different than it had higher up many dozens of steps ago.

At last they left the staircase and Alfie escorted the girls into the baggage hold.

Sophie surveyed the endless stacks of trunks and crates and whistled in amazement. "Who brought all this? The hatboxes alone would fill the Grand Canyon!"

"We can hardly be expected to travel without the necessities of life," said Juliana stiffly.

Sophie laughed. "How many hats did you bring?"

"Spring weather in New York can be unpredictable —"

"How many?"

"Eleven," Juliana said defiantly — and then giggled.

"And this is only first and second class," Alfie put in, leading them through the maze of baggage. He stopped at a tower of crates secured by netting and reached in through the slats of one marked *Galerie Gavroche, Montmartre, Paris*. They waited as he drew out the scrapbook and placed it on the flat side of a trunk before them.

Juliana was appalled. "You dare to rifle through people's belongings?"

"No, no! I found this! It must have fallen out of somebody's luggage. Please — take a look."

The girls began a slow perusal of the heavy pages, their faces twisting with revulsion at the description of such grisly crimes.

It dawned on Juliana first. "This is about the Whitechapel murders — the man they call Jack the Ripper!"

Alfie nodded eagerly. "So you've heard of him."

"Of course," said Sophie. "Even in America. Some stories are so awful that they never fade away. Especially since the Ripper was never caught."

"Exactly!" Alfie exclaimed. "This is *his* scrapbook. He's aboard the *Titanic*!"

"Don't be ridiculous," scoffed Juliana. "He's probably long dead. The murders stopped decades ago."

"Then how do you explain the scrapbook?" Alfie challenged.

"Why would you have to?" Sophie reasoned. "This book is a record kept by some person who was fascinated by the killings. It could belong to anybody."

"I don't think so," Alfie said gravely. "The details written in the margins — only someone who was there could know these things. And there are" — he hesitated — "souvenirs."

Juliana was wary. "What sort of souvenirs?"

"Look." He leafed forward to reveal a square of fabric obviously cut with a knife. "This piece of cloth comes from Annie Chapman's dress. I think the brown stain is old blood. It gets worse. There are" — he shivered — "human teeth. All displayed like it's something to be proud of."

Sophie's eyes were wide. "It still doesn't prove that we're dealing with Jack the Ripper. I admit it's someone loathsome — with a sick mind, who admires a rampaging butcher enough to create a scrapbook in his honor."

"And this person is *on board*?" Juliana demanded. "Not in first class, certainly!"

"Money doesn't stop a man from being horrible," Sophie reminded her gently. "Or a woman." Equality in every way — Amelia Bronson's motto.

Juliana looked haunted. "Whether it's the real Ripper or not, it's frightening! Whose book could this be?"

"I spend all my spare time down here, trying to learn exactly that," Alfie promised. "It must have fallen out of a torn satchel or an open trunk. When I find which one, it'll be tagged with a cabin number, and that'll tell me the name. Then I can alert the captain, and have the monster thrown in the brig."

The girls stared at him.

"Think of it," he went on. "When we steam into New York with Jack the Ripper behind bars, this ship will be on the front page of every newspaper in the world!" His eyes were shining with excitement. "People will be talking about the maiden voyage of the *Titanic* a hundred years from now!"

He was interrupted by a scraping sound. The wheel on the hatch to the fireman's passage began to turn slowly.

"Somebody's coming!" Alfie rasped.

CHAPTER EIGHTEEN

Alfie put a hand on each girl's shoulder and lowered all three of them into the shadowed hiding place behind a stack of luggage.

Juliana and Sophie hid their faces. But Alfie watched, barely daring to breathe, as a slender, compact figure stepped into the baggage hold. He saw the steward's uniform first, before the newcomer turned and light fell on his face.

Paddy Burns.

Alfie's first reaction was relief. This could just as easily have been Second Officer Lightoller on an inspection. Mr. Lightoller was a hard man, and the consequences would have been dire. What luck that the person who had stumbled upon them should be the one soul aboard this ship who dared not try to turn him in.

But there were complications. He couldn't let Juliana and Sophie learn that he was aiding and abetting a stowaway. That was a serious crime, far worse than sneaking two first-class young ladies down to the baggage hold.

Sophie got his attention and mouthed the words, "Who is it?"

"Another steward," Alfie whispered. "Just stay hidden."

As they watched, Paddy prowled the hold, checking luggage tags. Alfie looked around, plotting a line of retreat through the canyons of baggage. It would be so much simpler if Paddy never learned they were there.

The stowaway was only a dozen feet away and approaching, still checking tags.

"Should we run?" Juliana murmured, scared.

Alfie didn't dare answer. Paddy was that close. It was too late for escape, or even a different hiding place. All they could do was stay frozen and hope for the best.

Ten feet away. Then eight . . .

At almost the same instant, a cold hand from each girl squeezed Alfie's fingers. Paddy was almost upon them!

And then he stopped short. A small knife appeared in his hand, and he sawed a hole in the netting securing the baggage in front of him. A few seconds later, he withdrew a small trunk from the pile and started away with it.

"He's stealing!" hissed Juliana in anger.

"I'm sure he's just fetching it for one of his passengers," Alfie explained lamely. He knew this could not be true as surely as he knew that Paddy was no steward. What was the boy up to? He'd promised Alfie that he wouldn't steal, but what was the word of a stowaway worth?

Paddy set the trunk down in a clear spot under an electric light and began picking at the lock with the tip of his knife.

In scarcely an instant, the padlock was open and the lid lifted. Paddy began to rummage through the contents, searching for . . . what? Money? Jewelry? Then, inexplicably, he shoved everything back inside and slammed the cover shut. With great effort, he heaved the trunk up on his shoulder and maneuvered it to the spiral staircase. He began an unsteady climb.

As soon as he was out of sight, Juliana was on her feet. "We have to follow him!"

Alfie stared at her. "Why?"

"Because," she replied primly, "it is the duty of every good citizen to take action in the face of lawlessness."

"You're starting to sound like my mother," Sophie put in uneasily.

"I'm going to confront him," Juliana insisted. "The next piece of baggage he steals could be mine. Or yours."

She started for the spiral stairs. Sophie was right behind her.

With a groan, Alfie stuffed the scrapbook back into its hiding place and followed them. It was his fault the girls were here at all, and he couldn't let anything happen to them. He couldn't let anything happen to Paddy, either. Somehow, he had intertwined his fate with a group of strangers, and it was too late to untangle himself.

Stealthily, they listened to the vibrations of Paddy's footsteps on the metal stairs above them. Then, abruptly, the vibrations ceased.

"He stopped," Sophie whispered.

Alfie shook his head. "That's not it. He got off — at E Deck, I think."

The three sped up to E Deck. Alfie peered through the hatch just in time to catch a glimpse of Paddy struggling down the passageway with his burden.

Alfie made a snap decision. "This way," he said,

pointing in the wrong direction. His life would be so much simpler if he could get the girls back to their cabins. Then he could worry about what Paddy was up to.

"No," said Juliana. "I saw him. He's down this passageway."

Resigned, Alfie led the girls along the narrow, unadorned corridor.

"Where *are* we?" asked Sophie, scanning the stark white paint over plain metal fittings, rivets exposed.

"Crew quarters," Alfie whispered in reply.

An open door revealed a double row of bunk beds. A buzz of male conversation spilled out into the passageway. But luckily, no one noticed them slinking by.

Dead ahead, another passage crossed the ship abeam.

"Which way should we go?" Sophie asked anxiously.

Juliana hesitated uncertainly. From the port side, a cold draft blew relentlessly toward them. Almost as if —

"Could a window be open down there?" she asked.

They turned left, jogged around a bulkhead, and stopped in their tracks, gaping in amazement. The corridor wound past a staircase and widened into a small atrium — the reception area for boarding second-class passengers. A heavy hatch provided access to the embarkation gangway. It was wide open, and the black Atlantic sped by below.

Paddy knelt there, the lid of the trunk flipped back. He was pulling trousers and shirts out of it and flinging them overboard into the sea.

"Stop that!" Juliana commanded.

Paddy looked up, but the pace of his tossing never slackened. "Begging your pardon, miss, but see to your own plate."

Sophie was genuinely intrigued. "Very well — so you're *not* stealing. But what *are* you doing? Why would you risk arrest by taking some poor person's belongings only to drop them into the ocean?"

A darkness passed over Paddy's face. "This is no 'poor person.' He's a heartless assassin, he is. This stuff belongs to the gangster who killed my best friend. At least it used to." A ghost of a smile flashed across his young features as he flung some fine linen underwear into the night. "Now it belongs to the fish."

"Why should we accept the word of a thief?" Juliana demanded.

In answer, Paddy reached into the trunk and produced a large black pistol.

Both girls retreated behind Alfie.

"Come on, Paddy," the young steward urged. "Put that down."

"I'll do better than that, I will." Paddy tossed the weapon out the open hatch.

"You called him Paddy," Juliana accused breathlessly. "You *know* him!"

"Well, uh, yes, but —"

"When were you planning to share that with us?" Sophie demanded.

"Paddy isn't a member of the crew, strictly speaking," Alfie mumbled.

"What is he, then?" Juliana asked scornfully. "A stowaway?" Alfie's shamefaced look told the whole story. "He *is*! You're harboring a stowaway!"

Paddy looked at her defiantly. "How easy it is for you to point your finger at me, standing there in those fine clothes with a good dinner in your belly. And I'll wager those eardrops are real diamonds!"

Juliana's hands flew to her ears.

"You're right," said Sophie, almost kindly. "Neither of us has lived your life. Why don't you tell us about it?"

"Not much to tell, is there?" Paddy replied stiffly. "I had every right to walk away from a stepfather who mistook my face for a punching bag. Daniel and I may have been hungry in Belfast, but we looked after each other. Did we steal? That we did, because starving to death was the only other choice. And I'd be right there still, happy with my lot, if Kevin Gilhooley hadn't killed Daniel and tried to kill me, too." He smiled grimly. "The fact that Gilhooley had a ticket on the same ship I stowed away on — well, I guess that's just what they call the luck of the Irish."

Soft-hearted Sophie was liquid with sympathy, but Juliana's expression remained stone.

"And you expect us to believe someone who jettisons a man's property and leaves him without a change of clothes to put on his back?"

"Oh, no, miss," said Paddy in mock seriousness. "I would never be so hard-hearted." From the open trunk, he produced a snowy white dress shirt — the sole item remaining — and spread it out on the deck in front of him. Then, from his back pocket, he pulled a shiny Waterman fountain pen. Squeezing the rubber reservoir and dragging the nib across the fabric, he wrote a single word in indelible black ink. At last, he held up the garment to show the others:

MURDERER

He fluttered the shirt to dry the ink, then folded it neatly and placed it back in the trunk.

Alfie rushed over and closed the hatch. "Paddy, you're daft!"

Paddy turned to Juliana. "Well, fancy lady, I suppose you'll be wanting to report me to the captain now. Alfie knows where to look for me. Then they'll throw me in the brig, and Gilhooley can come and kill me at his leisure."

He hefted the trunk, which weighed almost nothing now, and walked past them into the depths of E Deck.

Sophie turned pleading eyes on her friend. "Julie, you mustn't turn him in! It could cost him his life!"

Alfie regarded her in trepidation. It was hard to judge what the girl might do. Certainly, anything that harmed Paddy would damage him as well. Juliana didn't seem like a cruel person. But she was so mired in the world of lords and ladies that she had no idea of the hard choices ordinary people had to make.

Finally, Juliana spoke. "I wish to return to my stateroom, please."

"Promise you won't tell!" Sophie persisted.

"At once," said the daughter of the seventeenth Earl of Glamford.

CHAPTER NINETEEN

RMS *TITANIC*
Friday, April 12, 1912, 8:05 a.m.

Black lines floated through Paddy's mind . . . pencil lines?

A long shape sharpened into focus — the *Titanic*! This was Daniel's sketch!

Yes, Patrick, Daniel's voice resounded in his head. *And you'd best take a good look at it.*

Do you think an hour ever passes that I don't? Paddy challenged. *What does it mean? Help me, Daniel! I'm not clever like you!*

Look harder! Daniel commanded. *You're clever enough to put your fingers on the purse of any man in Belfast! You have to open your mind.*

I can't!

"Open it!"

The sharp words cut right into Paddy's dream, punctuated by loud banging. He shifted his position in the front seat of the motorcar. It may not have been luxury accommodations for the swells in first class, but he had slept in worse places.

"Hush, Daniel," he murmured.

"*Open!*" roared the voice.

Suddenly, the automobile door was yanked wide, and Paddy tumbled out onto the floor of the cargo hold. He lay in a heap, blinking sleep out of his eyes, trying to focus on the sailor glaring down at him.

The man was older, red-faced, with an air of command. And definitely angry. "What are you up to, boy? Catching forty winks while the rest of us do our jobs?"

"N-no, sir!" Paddy stammered, his mind working furiously on an explanation of what he might be doing in the front seat of a Renault automobile in the cargo hold. Obviously, he wasn't catnapping on the job — he had no job. But the truth was even worse!

You're a brainless one, Paddy Burns! You should have known that you might slumber late after last night's adventure!

"I'll have you on my report for this!" the outraged sailor stormed. "You're not fit to wear that uniform!"

You have no idea, Paddy thought, quaking inwardly.

The tirade continued. "The company will dock your pay, just see if they won't. What's your name, boy?"

Paddy hesitated. Should he flee? A quick survey of the hold revealed two other seamen. Could he outrun all three . . . ?

Suddenly, one of the younger men began to curse.

The senior sailor wheeled on him. "You keep a civil tongue in your head!"

"Sorry, Chief. But we forgot to bring the cargo manifest."

The chief launched into a string of expletives far more colorful than the first, his angry words echoing throughout the hold and the lower decks. At last, he barked, "What are you waiting for? Go up to the quartermaster's office and get it. And be swift about it! We're already behind schedule, and the morning has barely begun!"

Paddy sensed his opportunity. "I'll fetch it for you, sir!" he offered quickly.

The red face turned back to Paddy. "You?"

"To make up for" — he gestured toward the car — "that."

The chief produced a pocket watch and glanced at it. "Go. *Run!*" He turned back to his men, muttering,

"The whelps they hire on these days! Barely out of their mothers' arms!"

Paddy dashed to the spiral staircase and pounded up the metal steps, grateful to leave the chief and his crew behind. The life of a stowaway, he was beginning to realize, became increasingly difficult as the voyage went on. The *Titanic* wasn't due in New York for five days. How would he ever keep himself hidden for so long? Especially with Kevin Gilhooley and Seamus on board.

His mind whirled as he hurried along. *Why am I rushing so? I don't have to bring him the cargo manifest or anything else! The devil with him! The devil with all of them!*

Yet the more he thought of it, the more it made sense to complete the errand. The last thing he wanted was for that crew chief to complain about a mysterious young steward sleeping in the cargo hold. That would set off alarm bells all around the *Titanic*. Paddy's life was hard enough without a ship-wide search for the boy who was impersonating a crew member.

Somehow, he had to find the quartermaster's office and bring the chief what he needed. But how was he to do that? The *Titanic* was a huge floating city, with nine decks, scores of passageways, and hundreds of rooms and compartments. He couldn't wander the halls pleading for directions. That would be as suspicious as sleeping in the motorcar.

Alfie! He would find Alfie, and his protector would tell him what to do. Even if the junior steward didn't know where to find the quartermaster's office, at least he could ask without drawing attention to himself.

He reached the forecastle, squinting in the bright sunlight. Blinding, it was. What a difference from the clouds and drizzle of Ireland and England — especially on the lofty decks that were reserved for first class. At this hour, Alfie might be delivering morning coffee and chocolate to the staterooms, or helping in the dining saloon. Paddy hoped he could run into the fellow without too much delay.

Sure enough, he spied Alfie atop up on the boat deck. And Alfie spied him — even from this distance, he could see the dismay on the young steward's face. Alfie hurried down the companion stairs, and Paddy started forward to meet him in the well deck.

"Paddy, have you lost your mind?" he hissed. "What are you doing out here?"

"I have to find the quartermaster's office."

"No, you don't!" Alfie rasped. "You have to disappear until we reach New York!"

"We have a bigger problem." In a low voice, Paddy recounted the story of how he was discovered sleeping in the Renault.

Alfie was horrified. "They *found* you? Now they know there's a stowaway on board!"

Paddy shook his head. "They think I'm just a steward who got caught kipping on the job. And they'll keep on thinking it as long as I bring them what they want — which is the cargo manifest. Now, where's the quartermaster's office?"

"The cargo manifest isn't something you can pick up and walk away with like a salt mill from one of the dining saloons," Alfie argued. "It's a record of everything aboard the ship. The Americans have to approve it before they let us unload. Do you think the quartermaster will just hand it over to the likes of you?"

Paddy bristled. "Well, I've no choice but to try, haven't I?"

Alfie thought it over. "I'll bring it to you."

"Did I miss the ceremony where you were promoted to captain?" Paddy demanded. "That looks like a steward's coat you're wearing, same as the one on my back. Why should they give it to you and not me?"

"I'm the one who can prove that he works for the

White Star Line," Alfie reasoned. "Who knows, I might have to sign for something so important."

"I'm not ignorant," Paddy said belligerently. "Daniel taught me well. I can write my name — or anybody else's!"

"But *my* name is the one on the complement of crew." It was Alfie's turn to be angry. "Do you think this is fun for me, Paddy? To abandon my passengers, lie to the quartermaster, and gamble my job to save your neck? I'm trying to *help* you! The least you could say is thank you!"

Paddy backed down, chastened. "You're right. Thank you, Alfie."

"We'll be sharing a cell in the brig if this doesn't work," Alfie said nervously. "Wait here, and try to look like you belong. If anybody asks, you're fetching bouillon for your passengers."

"Bouillon?" Paddy repeated. But Alfie was already gone.

Paddy took a step back and did his best to fade into the background. What was bouillon? Obviously some fancy thing the swells enjoyed. Part of being poor, he reflected, was that you didn't even know what you were missing.

He thought of the two first-class girls Alfie had brought to the baggage hold. All done up like angels they'd been, hung with jewels, smelling of perfume, and dressed in fabrics so shiny and colors so bright — Paddy had only seen the like on ornaments hanging from Christmas trees.

Never had he expected to rub elbows with such swells. In a way, he still hadn't. The dark-haired girl had regarded him with pity and fascination, the way you'd examine a rare bird with a broken wing. And the blond one, the one with the diamond eardrops? Well, her nose was so high in the air that she probably wouldn't have noticed him at all except to look at the evil stowaway. To her, Paddy was not a person; he was the sum of the crimes he'd committed. The subject of morbid interest, like the grisly scrapbook that so captivated Alfie.

In truth, Paddy had expected Juliana to turn him in to the captain. That had been his first thought when the crew chief had awoken him this morning. Yet somehow Alfie must have convinced her to keep silent. Bully for Alfie. He really was more than a soft-headed stoker's son with a wild imagination — someone to be blackmailed or manipulated. He was a friend.

The thought caught Paddy off guard. For more than a year, he had allowed himself to trust no one but himself and Daniel. But Daniel was gone, and this certainly wasn't Belfast. For good or ill, he had no choice but to trust in Alfie.

"I want hourly checks on the freshwater tanks. . . ." came a voice that crackled with stern authority.

And before Paddy had the chance to disappear down a companion stairway, two men rounded a corner and were upon him. One was in coveralls, blackened with soot from the engine room. The other wore the uniform of an officer — and an important one, too. Lightoller, they called him. Paddy had seen him on the bridge, next to Captain Smith himself.

"As the temperature drops, we don't want the lines to freeze," Second Officer Lightoller was saying, raising his collar to protect his ruddy features from the wind. Suddenly, he stopped, his alert eyes focused on Paddy. "And who might you be?"

Others would have panicked, but not Paddy Burns. He was used to living by his wits. "I'm waiting to escort a young lady to breakfast, sir."

Lightoller frowned. "I didn't ask what you're doing. I asked for your name."

"Junior Steward Alfie Huggins," Paddy replied readily.

"John Huggins is a fireman on the black gang," the coveralled man supplied. "His boy's a steward.

And I'll tell you, Mr. Lightoller, he's not Irish like this one."

Paddy was off and running before the second officer had a chance to react. He ducked inside the ship's superstructure and scampered down the forward first-class staircase. He could hear running feet at the top of the steps, along with Lightoller's voice: "Alert the bridge!"

Paddy got off at C Deck and snaked around the corner in a first-class passageway. He darted out to the promenade, sidestepped a young child playing with a hobbyhorse, and pounded aft, drawing stares from the handful of passengers on their way to breakfast. A companion staircase brought him down to D Deck, but no lower. The *Titanic* was laid out like a maze, designed to separate the three classes of service. It was easier to move from deck to deck than from fore to aft. Luckily, Paddy had been aboard before the ship had even taken on crew. He had used that time well, anticipating that a stowaway would need escape routes.

He paused, listening for signs of pursuit, and then found another staircase that led to E Deck. There, he made his way to Scotland Road, the longest passageway aboard. It was filled with crew, bustling this way and that as the largest ocean liner in the world began her day. Since he was in uniform, too, he blended right in.

Walking now, he moved briskly astern, marveling at the *Titanic*'s sheer length. It would have been a stroll of a full sixth of a mile, had he not climbed back up to D Deck via a maintenance ladder. Now he was in the second-class part of the ship. Nobody was chasing him anymore, he was pretty sure. But if Lightoller had notified the bridge that he was pursuing a young imposter in a steward's uniform, it was probably a good idea to avoid crew members as the word had a chance to spread. The intraship communications were the most modern in the world, with telephones in all main sections. News would travel quickly.

Running once again, he shot past the galley, bypassed the hospital, and was moving at a fast pace when he reached the reception room of the second-class dining saloon. So intent was he on the main entrance that he never noticed the door that was opening right in front of him.

The collision was so sudden, so shocking, that it took his breath away. Muffins and hot tea flew in all directions. A silver tray hit the floor with a clanging sound, punctuated by the crack of breaking dishes.

"Mind where you're going, you little —"

Paddy looked up into a glowering face with a misshapen nose that had been broken many times.

It was Seamus, Kevin Gilhooley's bodyguard.

CHAPTER TWENTY

RMS *TITANIC*
FRIDAY, APRIL 12, 1912, 8:30 A.M.

The huge man grabbed Paddy by his thin shoulders. The boy struggled, but could not break loose. Paddy's street instincts came to the fore, and he bit down hard on the henchman's wrist.

With a cry, Seamus let go. Paddy snatched up the teapot and broke it across his assailant's knees. This brought about more howling, along with some well-placed curses.

A waiter appeared in the main entrance. "Sir, I beg you! There are ladies in the dining —"

Another man appeared. Kevin Gilhooley.

Paddy fled as if he'd been shot from a cannon. Gilhooley shoved the waiter aside, knocking the man off his feet, and gave chase, Seamus hot on his heels.

Paddy's mind worked furiously. Was there anyone aboard this ship who wasn't after him?

There had been little hysteria in his escape from

Mr. Lightoller, but now Paddy's legs were fueled by raw fear. The tender mercies of the second officer seemed pleasant compared with what these two thugs had planned for him. They had murdered Daniel in cold blood, and Paddy was about to be next.

He scampered down the corridor past second-class cabins, dancing around a steward pushing a coffee cart. All at once, Paddy whirled around and gave the trolley a shove, sending it rolling toward his pursuers.

With a crash, the gangsters barreled into the cart, knocking it over and sending cups and saucers everywhere.

"Hey!" the steward exclaimed in outrage.

The two thugs ran right over him, leaving him dazed on the carpeting.

Running hard, Paddy risked a glance over his shoulder and was shocked to find Gilhooley and Seamus only a few strides behind. How could he ever get away from two men who plowed like steam-powered road rollers over all obstacles, human or otherwise?

E Deck! If he could get back to Scotland Road, he'd be safe. The Gilhooleys might be willing to trample a lone steward, but they could never attack him in a passageway teeming with sailors.

I'll be exposing myself to arrest by the White Star Line, but at least I'll have my life!

He leaped down the companion stairs, expecting to enter the busy thoroughfare favored by the crew. Instead, he found himself in a narrow corridor of more second-class staterooms. What was going on? Had he gotten confused and landed on the wrong deck?

He squinted at the cabin door. E-87. This was E Deck, all right. Where was Scotland Road?

Heavy footfalls rattled the companion stairs. His pursuers were almost upon him!

Paddy looked around desperately. Only one door was open — the second-class barbershop.

He raced past the bewildered shopkeeper and leaped into a barber's chair, sending it spinning. As it swung past the counter, Paddy reached into a bowl, coming up with a large dollop of shaving lather. He smeared the cream over his face with one hand while pulling a towel over his clothes with the other.

The barber stared in amazement. "Lad, I don't know what you think you're —"

Paddy looked up with terrified eyes and breathed a single word: *"Please."*

A second later, Gilhooley and Seamus roared down the passageway.

The barber must have understood. He stepped in front of the chair, shielding Paddy from the doorway. Picking up a straight razor, he pretended to shave his "customer."

Angry voices reverberated outside. "The little worm couldn't have gone far!"

Paddy shut his eyes and did something he hadn't done in a long time. He prayed.

And then the two men were in the shop, filling it with their presence.

"A nasty little whelp in a ship's uniform," Gilhooley called to the barber. "Which way did he go?"

"I saw no such person," the barber replied stiffly.

With a grunt, the gangster stepped out of the shop. All at once, Seamus grabbed his boss by the shoulder and pulled him back inside, indicating the mirror opposite the barber chair. There, from a mass of shaving lather, peeked the familiar face of a young boy.

Paddy was out of the seat in a flash, his sole hope a swan dive through the narrow space between the two thugs. He very nearly made it.

Seamus wrapped strong arms around Paddy, preventing all movement. It was impossible even to struggle. He cast a threatening look back at the terrified barber. "I'll be remembering how helpful you were."

Kevin Gilhooley addressed his victim. "Lovely day for a funeral, eh, boy?"

CHAPTER TWENTY-ONE

The cargo manifest was the biggest, bulkiest, heaviest, most unwieldy book that Alfie could have imagined. It took all his strength to lug it up the spiral stairs to where he'd left Paddy. How the smaller boy was going to manage to get it down to the cargo hold was a mystery.

He reached the forepeak, and then headed aft to the well deck, where Paddy was waiting.

Only Paddy wasn't waiting. He was gone.

Calm down, Alfie told himself, laboring to control his breathing. *He's probably just hiding from one of the officers. It's a good thing. It means he's got some sense.*

"Paddy," he called softly. "You can come out now. It's just me."

No answer.

"You can come out now. I've got the book."

He waited. *Come on, Paddy. You said you were in a hurry!*

Something was wrong. Alfie pondered his options. He could take the manifest down to the hold and hand it over. But what if the crew chief realized that this young steward didn't match the one he'd found in the car? Would that set off some sort of investigation?

Even more distressing, where *was* Paddy — and what trouble might he be getting into at this very moment? Trouble for Paddy meant trouble for Alfie, too. He had to find the boy. But where would he even begin to look aboard the largest moving object on the face of the earth?

The boat deck, he decided. At least from higher up, he could see more of the ship. If Paddy was topside, he would be visible from there. It wasn't much to go on, but at least it was something.

As he started up the companion stairs, he spied Sophie at the rail on the arm of Major Mountjoy. Sophie's eyes locked on Alfie's, sending a message of pure desperation.

"Alfie!" she called with high-pitched enthusiasm. Noticing the cargo manifest under his arm, she exclaimed, "You brought my book from the library! I'm anxious to begin reading it at once!"

"I say!" the major announced jovially, reaching for the leather-bound volume in Alfie's arms. "I must see what reading material has this exquisite young lady so entranced!" Alfie tried to hold back, but the portly major wrenched the book from him and began to leaf through it.

"Bless my soul!" the major exclaimed, staring at a bill of lading for three thousand tins of Norwegian sardines. "I confess that I do not comprehend what interests the young people have these days."

"Sardines are — all the rage in New York this season," Sophie ventured.

"Ah, yes. Your American fashion tastes," the major blustered. "Like that Turkey Trot one hears so much about. Well, I'll leave you to your reading, my dear." He sketched a bow that was remarkably low considering the size of his stomach, then waddled off.

Sophie smothered her laughter. "Oh, thank you, Alfie. What is that book?"

"The cargo manifest. Paddy needs it. Have you seen him?"

"Paddy?" She frowned. "What's he doing up here?"

Breathlessly, Alfie filled her in on the details. "I left him on the well deck, but he's not there anymore. I'm afraid he's gotten himself caught."

"I'll help you look for him," she decided. "We'll split up and meet back here. Don't worry, we'll find him."

"Thanks."

Alfie crossed over to starboard, and Sophie headed aft on the port side, gingerly trying doors and peering into every nook and cranny. As she passed through the shadow cast by the first towering smokestack, the brisk air became even colder, and she hugged her arms to her sides.

"Sophie!"

Juliana sat up in her deck chair, waving and beckoning. "What is it?" she called, noting her friend's furtive manner. Then, dropping her voice: "It's Major Muttonchop, isn't it?"

"Have you seen Paddy anywhere?" Sophie blurted.

Juliana's smile disappeared abruptly. She looked away from Sophie and gazed out over the Atlantic. "I'm sure I don't know what you're talking about."

"Maybe he hasn't had the advantages you've had, but he's a *person*, Julie!" Sophie said crossly. "And he could be in trouble."

Juliana was unsympathetic. "If he's in trouble, it's thanks to his own lawless behavior, which started the moment he stowed away aboard this ship! Frankly, I find it mystifying that you insist on becoming involved with this criminal and his problems. It's none of your affair, and it's unsavory for you to be entangled in this tawdry drama — all in an attempt to protect someone who does not deserve even one second of your attention, much less your protection!"

Sophie regarded her intently. "Julie, I like you a lot. But I just can't be friends with someone so heartless." And she ran off, continuing her search for the hapless Paddy.

☆

Kevin Gilhooley had chosen his bodyguard well. The brute strength of the man called Seamus was nothing short of superhuman. What appeared to be a friendly arm around Paddy's shoulders was as powerful as a yoke of iron. And the large hand that covered the boy's mouth pressed down with enough force to smother all sound. Never before had Paddy felt so entirely under the physical control of another. He did not entertain thoughts of escape. It was all he could do to breathe.

In this manner, Seamus brought him up the staircases and companionways of second class. Gilhooley opened the heavy door and ushered them into the cold wind and brilliant sunshine of the boat deck.

"Take a look around, boy," the gangster invited. "So much beauty in the world! A great pity it is that you'll not be here to enjoy any of it."

And look around Paddy did — with growing desperation. They were in the aftermost part of the boat deck, behind the fourth funnel, overlooking the stern. The area was deserted. He could make out a few hardy figures braving the wind far forward in the first-class section, and there were steerage passengers below in the aft well deck. But second class was lazy today, lingering in their cabins or finishing breakfast in the dining saloon.

Gilhooley's voice was as cold and cruel as the bite of the wind. "Do it, Seamus."

Now Paddy did struggle, although he knew it would be to no avail. Seamus dragged him toward the rail and grasped him under the arms in order to heave him up and over the side.

The instant his mouth was free, Paddy began to scream for help. Gilhooley tried to muzzle him, but Paddy bit down hard on the gangster's fingers. Gilhooley's bellowing was almost as loud as Paddy's, and the angry man lashed out, striking the frenzied boy repeatedly in the face. Paddy recoiled, tasting blood, but kept on shouting.

He was aware of his feet leaving the deck as Seamus

lifted him high. He saw the rail below him and knew that next would come the long fall, followed by a splash into icy black water. Reaching down, he clamped both hands onto the bar and held on.

If they want me in the sea, they're going to have to break all my fingers!

Gilhooley pounded at those small fists, but Paddy steeled himself and clung tightly. The pain was unimaginable, but the alternative was death. At the same time, he kicked out, landing a solid blow into Seamus's belly. With a cry of outrage, the henchman unleashed his full force. Paddy felt himself swing up and over. He was off the ship, clinging fiercely to the rail, nothing but thin air between him and the Atlantic.

In that wild instant, Paddy was no longer involved in the struggle, but merely a spectator. *How long can that boy hold on?* he wondered in a strangely detached manner.

Not very long at all. He was in agony, bone-weary, and his fingers were so cold. . . .

CHAPTER TWENTY-TWO

A large, leather-bound ledger swung out of nowhere and caught Seamus full in the face. The bodyguard staggered backward, blood pouring from a large nose that had been shattered yet again.

"*Help!*" Alfie bellowed, waving the cargo manifest to keep Gilhooley at bay.

The gangster's eyes narrowed with rage at the young steward. "You've made a grave mistake, laddie —"

But at that moment, running feet rattled the deck. Stewards and seamen converged on the spot from all directions.

"Call the master-at-arms!" Alfie shouted. He reached through the rail and grasped Paddy by the wrist. Try as he might, he lacked the strength to heave the smaller boy back aboard.

Crew members swarmed the spot, taking hold of Gilhooley and Seamus. Two sailors pulled Paddy up and over the side, setting his feet on the deck.

"Are you all right, son?" asked the older of the two.

In answer, Paddy turned tail and sprinted along the boat deck, leaving his rescuers staring after him, openmouthed. They had saved his life, and he was grateful, by God. But he was still a stowaway aboard this ship. And Paddy Burns had a talent for shifting his attention from one problem to the next with lightning speed.

He hurdled the gate into first class and hoisted himself onto the broad metal grid. As he scrambled across, he looked down on the stained-glass dome that covered the aft Grand Staircase. Jumping to the deck, he dodged his way through cranes and equipment, and raced forward, now on the starboard side.

He heard shouts behind him, and pounding footfalls. *Sure,* he thought bitterly, *two gangsters just tried to throw a fourteen-year-old boy overboard, but the White Star Line's chief concern is capturing me!*

There was no way he could hope to elude sailors on their own ship. He had to hide. *Now.*

He tried several doors along the superstructure — all locked. His eyes fell on the line of covered lifeboats. It would have to do.

He climbed up to the nearest one and slipped under the tarpaulin. Furtively, he peered out to check for pursuit.

The sailors had not appeared yet. But he was not entirely alone. There at the rail, staring straight at him, was the fancy girl with the diamond eardrops — the one who had looked at him with such contempt. There could be no question that she'd seen him — and also no question that she would turn him in. He was doomed.

He caught sight of the pursuers then and, coming from the opposite direction, a single imposing figure in an officer's uniform. Lightoller. Paddy ducked out of sight and secured the cover around the lifeboat.

"Report!" the second officer barked.

"We've got two in custody," a sailor called back. "A right nasty pair of cutthroats! They tried to throw the boy overboard!"

"Who's the boy?" Lightoller asked.

"A stowaway, we think. He was that anxious to get away."

Lightoller turned to Juliana. "I'm sorry to trouble

you, miss. Did you see this boy? I believe he's wearing a steward's uniform."

Paddy's heart sank. Well, here it was, the end of the road. He had been saved — but only to be delivered into the hands of the White Star Line. He waited for the girl to expose his hiding place.

"Yes, I did, Mr. Lightoller," he heard Juliana announce. "He was heading forward, toward the wheelhouse."

Paddy sat up in shock. Had the girl somehow overlooked him? No, impossible. She had watched him climb into this very lifeboat. Their eyes had met — he could still feel the sting of her scorn and disapproval. . . .

"Are you absolutely certain?" Lightoller persisted. "I came from that way myself, and I didn't notice anyone."

"Oh, yes," was Juliana's reply. "He was running very fast. Perhaps he crossed over to port, and you missed him."

Paddy could not believe his ears. This rich girl, who had more wealth dangling from one ear than he could ever hope to touch in a lifetime, was *protecting* him!

Why would she help him? No — this went far *beyond* help. She was lying to an officer, risking serious trouble. Aiding a stowaway was a *crime*!

"Perhaps he did," came Lightoller's voice again, although he did not sound convinced. "This way, men."

Paddy heard more running feet and then quiet. A moment later, a soft voice called, "Are you all right?"

He peered up at her. The judgment was gone from her eyes, but her expression did not seem friendly. She looked stunned, as if taking Paddy's side had been even more bewildering to her than it had been to him.

"Thank you for not turning me in, miss."

"Those men almost killed you," she said in horrified amazement.

Paddy tried to smile. "We Belfasters are a friendly lot." He began to swing his leg over the side. "I'll be on my way —"

"You'll stay right where you are!" she countered in a sharp whisper. "*I'll* tell you when it's safe to come down."

Paddy sat back in the curved bottom of the boat, hugging his knees to his chest. Quite an eventful morning, even by the standards of a Belfast street lad — nearly murdered, and then nearly arrested by his rescuers. And now this — a helping hand from the last person he'd ever imagined would offer one.

He patted his jacket, feeling Daniel's drawing against his heart. He would have given everything he had — which was nothing, mind you — to be back with his old friend in their abandoned print shop.

Yet a fellow can find support and kindness in this pitiless world. It's out there — even aboard a ship-load of millionaires.

You just had to look hard enough.

Still, Paddy knew his position was precarious. There was something about that Mr. Lightoller — the hardness of his expression, the unyielding steel of his eyes. The second officer would never rest until the stowaway had been captured and brought to justice.

He shifted, trying to fall into a comfortable position. Considering the size of the ship, the lifeboats were a lot smaller than he'd expected.

Yet, oddly, there didn't seem to be very many of them. . . .

CHAPTER TWENTY-THREE

The *Titanic*'s brig consisted of two small cells adjoining the office of the master-at-arms on E Deck.

It took Master-at-Arms Thomas King and four able seamen to escort Kevin Gilhooley and his bodyguard to what would be their quarters for the remainder of the voyage. Seamus alone, his long crooked nose dripping blood onto a sweater that had once been cream-colored, required no less than three men to force him inside and slam the gate.

Nor did the Belfast gangsters come along quietly. Down five decks and across half the length of the ship they struggled, blustered, and cursed, drawing horrified looks from three classes of passengers and an assortment of stewards and maids. Both prisoners were bruised and battered from their scuffle. Gilhooley gangsters were notoriously tough, but so were English sailors. And the crew held an overwhelming advantage in numbers.

"Why are you protecting that little scum?" Gilhooley raged as King locked the cell door. "A thief, he is. A common pickpocket!"

"I saw no thievery," King said severely. "The crime I witnessed was attempted murder most foul. And I'll see you hang for it, or I never sailed salt water."

"Does the name James Gilhooley mean anything to you?" the gangster persisted. "My brother runs Belfast, including the shipyards. If a true seaman you are, you'll face him eventually."

The master-at-arms was not intimidated. "And if that day comes, I'll tell him his brother got what he deserved for trying to throw a defenseless boy over the rail. Ah, there you are, Matherson —"

A tall, gaunt sailor entered the office carrying a small trunk.

"I took the liberty of sending for your luggage," King informed his prisoners. "You two look a disgrace — which is how hooligans are supposed to look, I suppose. But since we're destined to be together in this office for the rest of the crossing, I aim to clean you up a bit." He accepted the trunk and frowned. "Rather light, isn't it?"

He popped the latch, removed the lone shirt, and held it up for the prisoners. The ink-dabbed message stood out against the gleaming white linen:

MURDERER

Gilhooley shook the gate of the cell, howling like a madman. "You blithering fool, can't you see I've been robbed? What kind of ship are you running where miscreants put their mitts on a man's property and deface it with lies?"

"I see no lies," King replied evenly. "And the only miscreants are behind bars."

"My brother will hear about this!" Gilhooley bellowed. "I demand to send a wireless! Fetch me a form from the Marconi room! *Now!*"

"The Marconi facilities are for paying customers only."

"I'll pay," seethed Kevin Gilhooley, glaring at the master-at-arms through eyes that were barely slits. "And someday, so will you."

CHAPTER TWENTY-FOUR

BELFAST
Friday, April 12, 1912, 3:50 p.m.

Donovan's Bar and Grill on Victoria Street had not had a working kitchen since the turn of the century — ever since the restaurant had become headquarters for James Gilhooley and his organization. It was from this nerve center that the gangster oversaw a criminal empire that controlled the Belfast shipyards and beyond.

Many messengers came and went at Donovan's, but this one was greeted with suspicion. He was not one of the usual runners employed by Gilhooley. He was a representative of the Marconi Company, which sent, received, and delivered wireless communications. Thanks to Mr. Marconi's astonishing new invention, Morse code messages could be forwarded from ship to ship to ground station, reaching anywhere in the world in mere hours. It was just another way that the world had changed for the better in this incredible twentieth century.

"It's from the *Titanic*," the courier announced.

At the mention of the great ship, James Gilhooley himself rushed to the door and snatched the envelope, tossing a few coins to the man. "My baby brother's aboard her!" He ripped open the Marconigram and examined the paper, his face flushing with anger. "Damned if he isn't in jail!" he roared. "And Seamus, too!"

"Why would we expect better from the English?" growled the man behind the bar.

"It wasn't the English!" Gilhooley raged. "It was that little street rat! *His* partner!"

All attention in the room turned to the boy who was on his hands and knees on the floor, scrubbing with a wire brush.

Daniel Sullivan.

His eyes were still swollen nearly shut from the beating he'd received at the hands of this gang more than a week ago. By all rights, he should have been dead, and would have been. But the Gilhooleys had decided it was fine sport to keep him alive and turn him into an unpaid drudge and captive. For the past ten days, he had washed floors, cleaned water closets, and slaved over dishes and laundry for a group of men who taunted and tormented him at every turn. The men who had thrashed him and murdered Paddy.

Only Paddy *wasn't* dead! Daniel smiled as he scrubbed, ignoring the pain of a split lip. His friend had gotten away. Not only that, but he'd managed to land himself aboard the greatest ship in the world, right alongside Mr. Thomas Andrews himself. Better still, Paddy had been instrumental in having Kevin Gilhooley and his muscleman tossed in the clink.

As miserable as Daniel's lot had become, as bleak as his future might be, he still felt joy at the knowledge that his friend was sailing away toward a new life in America.

Nothing could stop Paddy now!

EPILOGUE

RMS *TITANIC*
Friday, April 12, 1912, 4:35 p.m.

On the forepeak, three elegant gentlemen stood in silent contemplation of the flawless sky and glass-smooth Atlantic. The ship beneath their feet moved effortlessly through the water. Never before had a liner cut the waves with so little vibration that one might mistake it for a building set on solid ground. The three were Thomas Andrews, designer of this magnificent vessel; J. Bruce Ismay, managing director of the White Star Line; and E. J. Smith, the most celebrated sea captain in the world. Even more rock-steady than the *Titanic* herself was the wealth of experience represented by this trio. No passenger could glance up at them without feeling a surge of confidence and pride that the maiden voyage could not be in better hands.

A uniformed crew member stepped onto the fore-deck and approached the captain. His name was Jack

Phillips, chief wireless operator aboard the *Titanic*. "A message from the shipping lanes ahead, sir. Ice has been reported above forty-two degrees latitude." He handed over a folded slip of paper.

"Thank you, Mr. Phillips." The captain accepted the note and slipped it into his pocket.

He did not read it.